CARIBE
Storm
The Valhalla Strike

ABSOLUTELY AMAZING eBOOKS

Habent Sua Fata Libelli

ABSOLUTELY AMA⚡ING eBOOKS

Manhanset House
Shelter Island Hts., New York 11965-0342

bricktower@aol.com • tech@absolutelyamazingebooks.com
• absolutelyamazingebooks.com

Library of Congress Cataloging-in-Publication Data
Craig, Bill
Caribe: Storm—The Valhalla Strike.
p. cm.
      1. FICTION / Mystery & Detective / Amateur Sleuth.
      2. FICTION / Mystery & Detective / General.
      3. FICTION / Thrillers / Suspense.
Fiction, I. Title.
ISBN: 978-1-949504-41-5 Trade Paper

April 2023

CARIBE
Storm
The Valhalla Strike

Book 5

Bill Craig

Also by Bill Craig

Key West Mysteries
Marlow: Indigo Tide
Marlow: Banana Wind
Marlow: The Neon Goodbye
Marlow: Mango Run
Marlow: Midnight Blues
Marlow: Something Wicked
Marlow: Dark Waters
Marlow: Papa's Legacy
Marlow: Hurricane Bay
Marlow: Lost Girl
Marlow: Red Tide
Marlow: Tropical Heat

Joe Collins Mysteries
The Butterfly Tattoo
Paradise Lost
Darkest Night

Circle City Mysteries
Chandler: Circle City Frame
Chandler: Circle City Shakedown
Chandler: Circle City Slam

The Fantastic Adventures of Hardluck Hannigan
Emerald Death
The Skymasters
River of the Sun
Curse of the Kill Devil

Decker P.I.
Scorpion Cay
Kill Shot

Caribe Mysteries
From Havana with Love
You Only Die Twice
Operation Skyfire
Operation Serpent's Tooth

Mitch Cooper Mysteries
One More Way to Die
The Past Never Dies
To Die For

Moseby and French Mysteries
Speaking For The Dead
Looking Into The Darkness

Storms Over Caldmy Series
The Gathering Storm
Storms Over Caldmy

Ravens Hollow: Wolf Moon
Jericho Walls: Texas Ranger
Maverick
Freetrader Orion

**Available from
AbsolutelyAmazingEbooks.com
and Booksellers**

Dedication

To Ian Fleming,
the father of the modern spy novel…

One

Nick Storm was lounging in a beach chair when the shadow passed over his face. Nick opened his eyes and glared at the person who stood above him blocking his sunlight. He was surprised when he recognized the man. "Jim King, how the hell have you been," Storm asked, sitting up.

"Doing well Nick. How about you? I heard that your agency was disbanded," King said. Jim King was six foot tall with longish blond hair and blue eyes. Nick had worked with him back in his CIA days.

"I'm enjoying being retired from the spy game," Nick replied sitting up. He grabbed a bottle of Killian's Red and took a long pull at the Irish Micro-brew.

"So, I heard. What are you doing these days?" Jim asked.

"Enjoying life. Why are you here, Jim?"

"I'm here because I need somebody I can trust. Something has come up and I need somebody from the outside to look into it," Jim sighed dropping into the chair beside Storm. A waitress came by and Jim ordered a Bud Light.

"I told you I'm retired, Jim."

"I know you did Nick, and that's why it has to be you. There's a mole in the Agency and they have managed to blow every operation we have sent into Costa Rica. Something big is going on down there. Plus, you already know the area."

"I do. What the hell, does the job pay?" Storm asked with a grin.

"It does. I'll have a contract drawn up and get you cover documentation and any hardware the job might require," King said as the waitress arrived with his beer.

Storm signed for the drink and billed it to his room. "To old times," Storm clinked his beer with Kings.

"To old times and new beginnings," King replied.

"So, where are you going to brief me on this?"

"I'll let you know. Keep your phone close," King drained his beer and then stood and walked away leaving Storm alone beside the pool.

Storm watched his old friend walk away and shook his head. Damn spies. They were worse than the Irish Republican Army and their whole *once in never out* policy. What the hell, he was getting bored anyway. While Caribe had officially been disbanded, Larry Dixon and Jack Riley both still lived on Key West. Nick figured it probably wouldn't hurt to talk to both of them and see what they thought about Jim King's offer.

~ ~ ~

"Are you sure you want to do this, Nick? You are out of the game now," Jack Riley shook his head.

"I am, but I am also bored to death. I need this Jack," Storm told his old boss.

"I can see that. I hate being forced to the sidelines myself, Nick. Larry and I will do whatever we can to help," Riley told him.

"Are you even going to ask him first?"

"I already did. He said yes. Did you expect anything different?"

"Not really," Storm admitted.

~ ~ ~

Two days later in Costa Rica…

Nick Storm stepped off of the flight from Key West and wasn't at all surprised that the air was just as thick as it had been on the island that he had left behind. Storm was still waiting for a briefing from Jim King, but so far, the CIA agent was curiously absent from any place that Storm looked.

Nick had one specially made suitcase with him that had come from Caribe. Riley had provided it because it allowed Storm to travel covertly with his Ruger 9mm and extra ammo and magazines for the pistol as well as a suppressor. It also allowed him to carry a boot knife and three throwing knives into the Central American country. Storm had also included a wire saw that could double as a garrote as needed.

San Jose airport was closer to the capital city of San Jose, which was Storm's primary destination. He was looking for a man, a scientist and virologist named Tristan Sorenson. Sorenson was working in a lab, supposedly doing research to prevent viral outbreaks, but he had disappeared from his lab, along with all of his research. Word had been leaked to the CIA and Jim had come to see him.

Now, Nick was in Costa Rica and he planned on checking into a hotel before heading to the lab to see what the hell had happened to Sorenson. The lab was expecting him in his cover identity of Aaron Wilkinson of the CDC. Alarms had sounded when Sorenson had vanished. Nobody wanted to talk about what he had been working on. That had triggered alarms all the way to the White House.

King was still supposed to meet him and give him a full briefing on Tristan Sorenson and what he had been working for. Since King felt that there was a mole in the Agency, Nick had decided to make his own travel arrangements and hotel reservation. He figured King would figure it out, but hopefully nobody else would.

Storm wanted to keep a low profile on this operation. He was still hurting over losing his team on the Bushman job. That had been a cluster fuck from the word go. Sometimes, he wondered what ever had happened to Cinder Ashe after she ended her time aboard *The Sea Chaser.*

It had been good to see Mackenzie and her crew, like the old days before Caribe. Before Kate. Kate Breton had been a British agent assigned to Caribe. She and Nick had developed a love/hate relationship the longer they worked together and had a physical affair that had ended because Nick had been a bit of a womanizer. Still, he had loved Kate. She had died along with another agent when a warehouse in Europe belonging to weapons dealer Andre Bushman when it had blown up.

From what Caribe Operations Director Jack Riley had been able to learn, Bushman's own people had triggered the explosion to wipe out evidence after Kate and her back-up had inadvertently tripped an alarm.

Riley had felt that it was a set-up, but had no evidence to prove it. Killing Bushman was one of the only times Nick had ever taken pleasure in a kill.

Nick pushed the memories away as he hailed a taxi outside the airport. He needed to look sharp right now, be aware of everything that was going on around him. For a spy, situational awareness was everything. Death could come from any angle at any time. He needed to be prepared to react if and when it happened so he could keep himself alive.

Working in a foreign country was always dangerous, and when that country was constantly in a fight with a neighboring country over international boundaries made it even more dangerous. Lots of times, guerilla terrorists would strike at prominent government targets deep in what was for them enemy territory. A whole lot of innocent bystanders had died because of it.

Using his dark-lensed sunglasses as cover, Nick scoped out the traffic around them as the taxi moved through the city towards his hotel. Nobody seemed to be paying any particular attention to his taxi, but Storm knew that didn't mean anything. There were any number of techniques that could be used to track him when he left the airport.

Personally, Nick thought that he had made it in country unobserved. But he was experienced enough to know that it wouldn't last. Especially when he started asking questions about Tristen Sorenson.

Nick figured that would heat things up in a hurry. There was evidence, according to Kim King, that Sorenson had not disappeared under his own power. To Nick, that meant that he had probably been kidnapped so that somebody could get their hands on whatever the hell Sorenson had been working on. More than likely, whoever had taken him wanted to weaponize his work. Storm didn't see the guy willingly going along with that.

The best spies tried to remain unnoticed in the background, just another grey face in the crowd. It required the ability to become a chameleon in a crowd. I had used that to my advantage so far. Storm hoped to continue to do so.

Storm picked a hotel at random, deciding on the Hotel Barceló San José

CR 10107. The rates were cheap, especially for it having a five-star rating. Storm rented a room under the alias of Nicholas Fury, and then took his luggage to his room. He didn't figure it would take too long for Jim King to find him.

Storm suspected that his CIA contact was already in-country and waiting for him. King had never been one to follow protocols to the letter. No, Nick was sure that king already had him spotted. The question was, if it was a good thing or not? King had been known to burn an asset to see what crawled up out of the sewer to take the asset down.

Nick had never liked being staked out as sacrificial bait. He quickly removed his Ruger ECS 9mm from his luggage and affixed the suppressor to the muzzle. He jacked a live round into the chamber, and then he settled in to wait. If he was right, trouble was headed his way. If he was wrong, then Jim King might get a nasty surprise.

Nick Storm closed the blinds and then positioned himself in a chair across from the door, his Ruger in his hand. The Ruger ECS was perfect for clandestine work. In size and weight, it was no larger than the Walther PPK, but it fired a full-blown 9mm cartridge. Storms was loaded with Federal 124-grain hydro-shok hollow-points. There was a core in the center of the bullet that would cause maximum expansion when it hit the target, causing catastrophic wounds in whatever it hit.

Storm had waited two hours when there was a knock on his door. He waited, the Ruger now at full-extension and locked on the center of the door. A second later, he heard the lock release. The door started to swing open. "You better be friendly," Storm said softly.

Jim King stood in the doorway, one hand holding a key card in the air and the other hand empty as it also reached for the sky. "Come on in and close the door," Storm told him. King complied. Storm dropped his hands holding the pistol into his lap, but where it could be brought into play right away if needed.

"I expected you before I left Key West," Nick told him.

"I would have if I could have but events didn't play out that way."

"So, what now?"

"I have creds that will get you into Sorenson's lab. You know where it is?"

"I do. I've done my homework, Jim."

"I never said you didn't."

"I know that."

"You know more than you are telling me, Jim. I need to know what it is or I turn around and fly back to Key West," Storm shrugged his shoulders.

"Nick, have I ever told you how much of a pain in my ass that you are?" King asked.

"Often, Jim. If you want me to do this for you, then you had better fucking play it straight with me. Fuck me and I'll fuck you back in ways you can never imagine," Storm told him.

"Sorenson was working on a virus, one that could be weaponized," King sighed.

"I thought we didn't do that sort of thing anymore," Storm sighed.

"Normally, we don't. This particular virus was developed in China and let loose on the public. A lot of people have died from it already."

"Covid-19?" Storm asked.

"The initial strain, yes. But Sorenson was working on a mutated strain. One far deadlier than the original."

"Omnicron?"

"Yes. Except Omnicron wasn't as long-lived as the Delta variant. It was more contagious, but it died off just as quickly."

"So, what are we looking at?" Nick asked.

"A brand-new virus, one ten times deadlier than Covid. It was code-named Valhalla. It has a 90% fatality rate. If this bug gets loose on the world, well we could be looking at end of days if it were to spread into a world-wide pandemic," King sighed.

"That could certainly be a problem," Storm nodded.

"No shit, Sherlock. That's why I need you to find and recover Sorenson before the new bug can be weaponized," King told him.

"Do you have any ideas as to where he might be?" Storm asked.

Maybe near Limon. That's where his lab was located."

"A secluded area then?"

"Yes, very secluded. Valhalla is highly contagious. It seemed safer to isolate the lab as far as we could from civilization. Limon isn't a major population center, despite being the 7th largest city in Costa Rica."

"You should have considered Antarctica," Storm told him.

"I did, but Sorenson refused."

"Of course, you did. So, when did the scientist disappear?"

"About a week ago. He had just notified Washington that he had found a way to weaponize the virus," King admitted.

"And he disappeared right after that?"

"He did."

"That cannot be good news. So, who do you think took him?" Storm asked.

"I have no idea. However, we need him found. Sorenson is the key to everything. If the bad guys get him, they can wipe out most of the population on the planet. We need to find this guy, Nick," King told me.

"I get that. The question is how? Do you have any suggestions, Jim?"

"No, I don't," King replied with a sigh.

"The you need to back off and let me work this. Can you get me into the facility?" Storm asked.

"I can. Give me until tomorrow and I'll have you a fully back-stopped identity package to get you inside."

"I'll see you then," Storm told him.

Two

Nick Storm shook his head. This mission was shaping up to be a clusterfuck of the first order. Nick knew it, as did his handler. Nick also knew that was why he had been sent in. Nick was expendable as far as the CIA was concerned. They used him for cannon fodder. Other agents were in play to take over if he should be killed. Except Nick had no plans of being killed.

Wuhan China was becoming a problem of the highest order. The way Storm figured it, the U.S.A. needed to nuke the place and wipe it off the face of the earth. However, that wasn't his call to make. So, instead he was in Costa Rica looking for Tristan Sorenson.

The problem was that Sorenson's lab wasn't located in San Juan, but 71 miles away in Limon. That meant that meant that Nick would need to travel to reach the lab. The question was what would he find when he got there? That was a question that Storm had to answer.

He didn't know what to expect, and so far, King had no answers for the questions that Nick had. That was why Nick had kept in touch with Riley and Dixon. He had far more trust in his old Caribe team mates than he did with the CIA.

Nick had been burned by the CIA before. He didn't plan for it to happen again. No, instead he planned on getting ahead of any interference that the CIA might throw his way.

The city of San Jose had a population of over 333,000, so it was a pretty sizable city. Nick wondered where in the name of God he was supposed to start looking for Tristan Sorenson? According to what King had told him, the guy was working at a lab 71 miles away, and that seemed a pretty long commute for twice a day. It had him wondering if he might do better by going directly to Limon. It only had a population of under 100,000 people. Still a needle in a haystack, but at least it was a smaller haystack.

What was the real reason Jim King had asked him to take on this job? Other than he was both outside the Agency and totally expendable? Nick had no answer, but he was sure there was a reason. Jim King rarely did anything without a reason. A mole in the Agency? That was certainly possible, but Nick felt that there had to be more to it than that.

It was something that he would have both Larry Dixon and Jack Riley check on. Riley had his own history with the CIA, not all of it good. But he would know who to talk to and what questions to ask. Nick would see what he could find out from Jim King in the meantime.

It was a balmy tropical afternoon with temps in the mid-seventies and low humidity despite the tropical location. With Panama to the south and Nicaragua to the north, Costa Rica was caught between two important countries. Costa Rica had no standing military presence and hadn't since 1948 after a bloody civil war.

However, given its location and porous borders, Costa Rica was a hotspot for drug and weapons smugglers. Terrorists also used it to transport members into and out of the United States, as well as other neighboring countries. In other words, Costa Rica was the Wild West of spy world. And that was where Nick Storm found himself.

Nick knew that eventually he would have to go to Limon, but would it be sooner or later? He had no idea. Jim King was supposed to deliver him a fully back-stopped identification package to get him into the lab. The question was, how fully was it back-stopped.

Not knowing how long it would take for King to get back, Storm decided to check out the city of San Jose. San Jose is not only the capital of Costa Rica but the largest city in the country. San José is notable among Latin American cities for its high quality of life, security, level of globalization, environmental performance, public service, and recognized institutions. According to studies on Latin America, San José is one of the safest and least violent cities in the region.

Not wanting to be caught with a gun, Nick clipped his tactical pen in his shirt pocket and his assisted-opening knife into his pants pocket. He had a small digital camera hanging from around his neck as he left the hotel and hailed a taxi. He told the driver that he wanted to see the sights. As the taxi pulled away, unfriendly eyes watched it go. The man pulled out into the traffic and followed the taxi at a discreet distance.

Storm snapped the occasional photo with his digital camera from inside the taxi. He had no desire to get out into the crowds of people that filled the sidewalks. No, Storm wanted to make any watchers come to him. So, here he was, riding around in a cab acting as bait with no way to shoot back if the other side had guns. Nick figured he would just have to make do with whatever hand he was dealt.

They rode around for a couple of hours before Nick decided to call it quits and return to his hotel. He paid the driver and stood outside in the late afternoon air watching the heartbeat of the city around him. Nick noticed a car pull up on the next block.

The thing about counter-surveillance was that it wasn't totally perfect. But Nick was fairly certain that he had spotted the car behind him a few times during the last two hours. Fortunately, his sunglasses masked his eyes so the driver didn't know that Storm was focused on him as he climbed out and starting heading Storm's way. Nick raised the digital camera and snapped a picture of the guy. He would e-mail it to Dixon later.

Storm turned and started walking back towards the entrance to his hotel. He could feel the guy moving closer and the short hairs on his neck were standing up. The guy was coming to kill him. Nick could feel it. That meant, he would need to have to react, to defend himself without cluing his attacker that he was anything more than a photographer on vacation in Costa Rica, which was the legend that Dixon had set up for him before he had left Key West to head south.

Nick took his time as he drew his tactical pen and palmed it in his right hand. It would be easier to confuse and witnesses into thinking that he was unarmed when he took the guy out. Nick moved through the crowded sidewalk feeling his target pushing closer to him through the crowd at his back.

Storm slowed his stride, giving the man at his back time to catch up. Storm glanced back over his shoulder and then rammed the barrel of the tactical pen into the man's diaphragm. The follower doubled over and fell to the sidewalk. Storm kept walking, quietly tucking the pen back into his pocket. He pulled out his phone and turned and snapped a picture of the guy as two good Samaritans were helping the man to his feet. Storm darted inside a department store and lost himself in the mass of shoppers that crowded the place.

Using all of his skills for shaking a tail, Storm made his way back to his hotel and man aged to slip inside to his room without encountering anyone. After shutting and locking the door, Storm quickly cleared the room and booted up his laptop. He wanted to talk to Riley and Dixon as soon as possible. Jim King was one of the few people that knew Nick Storm was in San Juan. That made him, at least in Storm's eyes, a suspect.

Once the encrypted laptop was booted up, it took another 30 seconds for the Zoom call to Key West to connect. "Nick, what's going on?" Jack Riley asked. As the former head of the Caribe task force, Riley looked older now. More gray in his hair.

"Somebody just tried to kill me out on the street. I dropped the guy using non-lethal force and walked away, but I got a picture." Nick pulled out his phone and pulled up the photo and hit send. "Sending it now."

"Got it," Larry Dixon chimed in a moment later. "Putting it in through facial recognition now. But Nick, it may take a while."

"I know, Larry. Jack, what were you able to find out about Jim King and this mission?"

"The mission is legit. The scientist, Tristan Sorenson is a specialist in microbiology and virology. He was working to fight a vaccine to stop a virus mutated from Covid-19 that is 100 times more deadly. Sorenson had named it Valhalla, and according to what he had told the CDC in Atlanta, the fatality rate was 95%. Sorenson was close to finding an antidote or vaccine to fight Valhalla. He had just sent that update the day before he had disappeared," Riley explained.

"King had sent another agent, Aaron Sparks to Limon to check out the lab. Sparks never reported back and two days later Sparks was caught up in a fishing net off the coast of Limon."

"That doesn't sound good," Storm sighed.

"Jim King appears clean, but I'll give him another go round given the attack on you," Riley told him.

"Thanks. I appreciate it, Jack," Storm said as he ended the call. Dixon would call him back when he found something. San Juan was becoming too hot to stay around. It looked like Nick was getting ready to head for Limon. What would be the best way? Flying would be fastest, but also more dangerous if the opposition had ground to air missiles. Driving the 71 miles would be equally dangerous. That left the train.

Storm picked up the phone and dialed the train station and secured a ticket to Limon. It was a smaller town that San Juan, but it was still a big place. Just then there was a knock on the door. Nick grabbed his Ruger 9mm and walked to the door. He took a cautious look through the peep hole in the door. It was Jim King.

Storm kept his pistol ready as he unlocked the door and stepped back as Jim King entered. King noticed the pistol right away. "Expecting somebody else?" King asked, raising an eyebrow.

"Somebody tried to kill me earlier. Got any ideas why that might happen?" Nick asked softly.

"None at all. But it does make me even more certain that there is a mole in the Agency," King sighed.

"No shit, Sherlock," Storm shook his head.

"No shit, indeed. Listen, Nick, are you absolutely sure you want to do this?" King asked, his face pale.

"Valhalla needs to be found and secured or life on the planet could be wiped out. Right now, it seems, I'm the best bet for making that happen. That bug cannot be allowed to fall into the wrong hands," Strom sighed.

"Here are your cover identity and travel papers as well the address of Sorenson's lab in Limon. I know that you've memorized my number already just in case. Those will get you inside the lab and cooperation from the people working there. Good luck, Nick," King told him, extending his hand. Storm shook it and then watched as King left.

Storm locked the door behind the CIA agent and walked back to the room's desk. He opened the envelope and acquainted himself with his new identity of Nathan Simms of the CDC. The documentation was some of the best he had ever seen and he took time to carefully read through it and memorize the background details. That was the part that tripped most operatives up. Not knowing the small throw-away details of their legend. Nick had learned that the hard way.

Storm hide his normal identifiers inside a secret compartment of his suitcase that couldn't be detected. His weapons were hidden there as well. He was paid up at the hotel until noon the next day. Taking his suitcase, he made his way to the parking lot and hailed a taxi. It took him to the train station.

The jungle train to Limon always left at 11:00a.m. The cost of the journey was around two dollars unless wanted to take first class accommodations. They were a bit more expensive but included better carriages than the second class. Storm figured that Nathan Simms would choose the first-class option.

The track offers a splendid introduction to the magnificent jungle-clad mountain landscape of Costa Rica. The line, with its 100 miles of embankments and dizzying trestles, took 20 years to complete. Malaria, dysentery and heat exhaustion are said to have buried 4,000 men who worked on it, Chinese, Italians and Hondurans - more even than the cutting of the Panama Canal - and only the laborers brought over from Jamaica proved strong enough to survive the punishing work. But when the track was opened, it shortened the trip to Europe, which had until then included a trip round Cape Horn, by three months.

Today the journey from San Jose to Puerto Limon on the Atlantic coast takes a little more than eight hours by train and even less - four to five hours - by air-conditioned bus. There is another railroad line that links San Jose to Puntarenas on the drier Pacific shore, but the Puerto Limon run is the voyage of choice, slicing through the uplands, past the white-water meanderings of the Rio Reventazon to the muggy coastal swamps until it reaches the Atlantic.

Storm had paid the $55.00 for the first-class ride. Each car held 24 passengers and had both fruit and ice chests full of beer. Storm had taken a seat at the rear of the car so that he could see all of the other passengers in his car. This also allowed him a perfect view of the jungle scenery that surrounded the track.

Nick had settled in to wait out the ride. He hoped that there was not another assassin waiting on the train, but there was no way that he could be sure. Nick needed to remain alert as possible during the eight-hour train ride. He figured that he could rest once he was in Limon.

The ride was not a fast one, but it was one that was filled with beauty. The rainforest held an exotic and dangerous beauty. Death lurked out there in the form of venomous snakes, deadly spiders, jaguars, poisonous plants. That was what had made the building the train tracks so deadly. A few thousand workers had died building the rail line to the Atlantic Ocean.

Three

Nick had made his way down to the front and grabbed a cold beer and some fruit about halfway through the trip. It had also given him a chance to familiarize himself with his fellow passengers faces. For the most part, they appeared to be rich tourists, but there were a few that appeared to be business people. None of them gave off the assassin vibe. Nick supposed that was a good thing, though he didn't let down his guard.

Nick pulled out his cell phone and started scrolling through it, checking his e-mail. There was nothing new there. He checked on the international news headlines but there was nothing of interest there, at least nothing pertaining to his mission.

Finally, feeling another need to stretch his legs, Storm made his way to the restroom and afterward decided to check out the other two first class behind his. The air outside was thick and humid, but after spending a few years on Key West, it didn't bother him. He stepped from the platform on his car to the next one. He waited a moment before opening the door and stepping inside.

The layout was the same as his own car, but there seemed to be less tourists and more business people   Some of them gave him surprised looks, others avoided his eyes as he walked back among them. That wasn't unusual in Central America. Often, meeting someone's eyes was regarded as a challenge. While Nick had no desire to challenge anyone, if someone wanted to challenge him, he would meet them head on. That was his preferred method of doing things.

It had gotten him in trouble on occasion, but it had gotten him out of it more often than not. Nick projected an aura of confidence as he made his way through the train car. Nobody seemed all that interested in him as he stepped outside and moved to the next car.

There were only about five occupied seats in this car, and the people looked a bit rougher than those in the other cars. He wasn't even sure that they had paid the high price to ride in the luxury car. A moment later, he was sure of it.

One of the closest guys lurched out of his seat and came toward him. Nick feinted with his fists and kicked the guy in the balls hard enough to lift his body six inches in the air. The guy went down for the count. Two others charged, trampling their compatriot on the floor. Storm punched the first guy in the throat and then caught the guy behind him in a rolling hip lock. The man behind him started to draw a gun, but Storm was quicker and his knife hit the man in the chest, piercing his heart. The fifth man spun and raced out of the car.

Storm let him go. He headed back to the one surviving member of the group. The only one still alive. Storm wiped the blade of his knife on the man's clothes to clean it. He placed the tip at the man's throat. "Who hired you?" Storm asked.

"Some guy back in San Jose. He wanted us to make sure that you didn't reach Limon alive," the man told him.

"Looks like you failed in that," Nick told him.

"Sometimes that happens," the man shrugged. Then he bit down hard and his mouth began to foam. Nick stepped back, recognizing the almond-like smell of cyanide. These guys were playing for keeps. Storm whirled around and slowly made his way back to his seat in the first car. This was the second attempt on his life in the past 24 hours. It was becoming very clear that somebody did not want him to complete the mission of finding and recovering Tristan Sorenson and his research.

A weaponized virus would be worth billions in the hands of any major or even minor terrorist group. Or any enemy country that hated the United States. Such group or country could kill off most of the world's population if they didn't understand exactly what they had.

There was no way in hell that Nick could let that happen. No, this meant that the mission was very real and the clock was ticking on the job. Surprisingly, there was no outcry about dead bodies being removed from the train when it finally reached Limon. In fact, there was no police presence at all when the train arrived. Storm took his suitcase and left the terminal as quickly as possible without drawing attention to himself.

Limon is the seventh largest city in Costa Rica and is the main Caribbean port. The population is largely creole and black population. Many of their ancestors had been brought to Costa Rica by slave ships. Per capita, Limón is the most violent province in Costa Rica. While violence is focused around the provincial capital, also called Limón, crime has spilled over to other parts of the province.

Organized crime has grown more powerful in Limon that in other parts of the country. That was one reason why it had been selected as a location for Sorenson's covert laboratory and research facility. Criminals had been paid handsomely to leave the building, and Sorenson, alone.

That meant that the local crime bosses would also be very interested in whoever had snatched the scientist out from under their noses. His disappearance had cost them money. That wasn't something that they would be willing to let pass. Storm sighed, figuring he would have to deal with them soon enough. He caught a taxi and took it to the Hotel Playa Bonita. It was a nice place and rather inexpensive. He took a regular room with both a full and twin bed. It had complementary WIFI as well.

Nick checked into his room and did a quick sweep for bugs before pulling out his laptop and sending a Zoom request for Jack Riley and Larry Dixon. He had also scanned a couple of local news outlets and there was still nothing about bodies being found on the train. That could mean one of two things. The bodies had been removed before the train had arrived in Limon, or the organization behind it had paid off local authorities. At this point, it was impossible to tell.

The Zoom call connected and both Riley and Dixon appeared in split image on the laptop screen. "Hey guys," Storm greeted the pair.

"What's happening, Nick?" Riley asked.

"I had five guys try to kill me on the train to Limon, but there was no alert about bodies being found on the train," Storm explained.

"Sounds like whoever is behind this is very good," Dixon cut in.

"I figured that out already," Storm rolled his eyes.

"I bet," Riley chuckled.

"I'm not sure if I should trust the legend King set up for me or not, but I need to get into that lab. Suggestions?" Nick asked.

"They don't know about you at the lab yet, so what King provided should be good for now. Larry and I'll get some replacement documentation ready in case you needed. Be careful, Nick," Riley told him. Storm ended the call and shut down the laptop.

Since Limon was on the seamier side of Costa Rica, Storm put his Ruger EC9 in the pocket holster and slipped it into his right-hand pocket. His tactical pen was in his shirt pocket, and his ASP expanding baton was in his left pocket along with his phone. Nick locked the laptop into the room's safe and then headed outside to call a cab.

~ ~ ~

The ride to the lab took half an hour as it was outside the city and a few miles out, sitting right on the coast. The taxi dropped him at the front entrance. Storm took a deep breath and let it out slowly, and then he walked up to the front door and entered, moving into the lobby of the lab.

The air-conditioning felt downright cold compared to the outside. Nick felt the goosebumps rising on his skin. He stepped towards the reception desk. Nick drew out the ID that King had provided him with. He flashed it at the gal at the reception desk.

Nathan Simms was quickly shown to a VIP suite to wait on his liaison to the laboratory. He didn't have to wait long before a gentleman who identified himself as Dr. Wilhelm Bergdorf entered the room.

Dr. Bergdorf was tall and thin with graying hair and cold blue eyes. That he was well into his sixties was very evident from his appearance. He also looked very tired. It wasn't hard to imagine why. Valhalla was dangerous. Since it and Dr. Sorenson were both among the missing, Bergdorf probably wasn't sleeping much. Maybe Storm could use that in his favor.

"Nathan Simms of the CDC, Dr. Bergdorf. I suppose you know why I'm here?" Storm asked. He looked at the scientist expectantly, waiting for the other man to speak.

"I assume you are here about discuss the disappearance of Dr. Sorenson and his research," Bergdorf replied, sweat beading on his forehead despite the air conditioning. Bergdorf removed his glasses and breathed on the lenses before polishing his with his silk handkerchief.

"You assume correctly. Can you tell me who authorized Dr. Sorenson's research?"

"I had assumed it was your government."

"You assumed mistakenly. Do you know what assume means, Dr. Bergdorf?

"What do you mean?"

"It means that when you assume, it will make an ass out of you or me," Storm glared at him. "How long had Sorenson been missing before you sounded an alarm?"

"Two days," Bergdorf muttered.

"So, whoever took him had at the least a 48-hour head start? Is that what you are telling me?" Storm asked.

"Yes," Bergdorf sighed.

"Do you know how far along Sorenson was in his research?"

"He had found a way to vector the virus into a weapon."

"When did that happen?"

"The night before he disappeared. He had sent me an e-mail to that effect."

"Did anyone else know?" Storm asked.

"I didn't tell anyone, but I have no idea whom Sorenson might have told," Bergdorf sighed.

"I need to see all of the surveillance footage from the night that Sorenson disappeared."

"I will arrange it," Bergdorf sighed.

"I hope so," Storm told him.

~ ~ ~

Two men stood at the edge of the jungle and watched the building that housed the laboratory. They used binoculars to survey the building. They had seen the man who was supposed to be from the Center for Disease Control enter the building. Their employer wanted to know everything they could find out about this man. Hopefully, Bergdorf would be able to give them more information after the man had left.

Arturo Diaz pulled out his cell phone and dialed his boss. The call was answered right away. "The man from the CDC is here," he told his employer.

"Keep an eye on him," the Boss told him before hanging up. Arturo nodded before putting his phone back in his pocket. "We are to follow this man," Arturo told his partner.

"Is that all?" Diego Montez asked, glancing at his boss.

"For now," Diaz replied.

~ ~ ~

Looking at surveillance tapes is one of the most boring jobs in the world. It made Storm wish he could send the digital files to Larry Dixon so the computer whiz could scan them with his vast array of programs. But that was impossible in this case. For one thing, Caribe no-longer officially existed, and for another he had no way to copy or upload them to the internet.

Storm sighed. He had been watching the tapes for a couple of hours and hadn't seen anything to indicate that Sorenson hadn't left under his own power. There had to be something that he was missing, but what? Nick paused the playback and rubbed his eyes.

This was a mind-numbing part of the job that Storm hated. But it had to be done. Either Sorenson had left on his own, or somebody had taken him. But which? Nick wished he still smoked, but realized it likely would not be allowed in here. He pressed play again and settled in to watch more of the tape.

It was more than an hour before he finally spotted something. Four men approached the rear loading dock at the lab building. All were masked and they all carried weapons. Nick leaned forward. This was definitely what he had been looking for. Storm clicked through all of the cameras and their feeds, following their progress through the building all the way to Sorenson's lab.

Storm pulled his iPhone out starting filming what was on the screen. He would send it to Dixon when he got back to his hotel. As he watched, the armed men busted into Sorenson's lab and knocked him down before handcuffing him. One man stood guard over him while the others ransacked his files, stealing a number of them. Storm figured those contained most of the data on Valhalla. Once they had everything, they dragged the scientist out of his lab, carrying boxes of files with them.

Storm videoed them leaving and was able to get a peek at the vehicle that they had loaded Sorenson into. It was a dark-colored SUV and he got a partial plate. He would send it all to Dixon to see what he could make of it.

Having gotten what, he needed Storm plugged the tapes back to the beginning. Tristan Sorenson had been kidnapped. Now the question was by who. That was what he was here to find out.

Bergdorf seemed relieved when Storm exited the building. The manager of the lab had been uncomfortable from the time Storm, in his Nathan Simms persona, had arrived at the lab. Storm climbed into the waiting taxi for the ride back to Limon.

Nick had learned a lot, probably more than Bergdorf had wanted him to. It was clear, however, that the Lab Manager knew that Sorenson had been taken. There was no other explanation.

Four

The drive back to the hotel was uneventful. Something for which Nick was thankful for. Things had been crazy from the day that Jim King had shown up and invited him into this mess. Nick headed for his room, but he maintained situational awareness.

Spies always needed to be aware of their surroundings. That was what kept them alive. It was for him, anyway. Storm took the stairs up to his floor. He took a peek through the window in the stairwell door. The hall was clear. Storm slipped out of the stairwell and headed down the hall to his door. One quick swipe of the key card and the lock clicked open. Storm stepped inside.

"What did you find out?" Jim King asked from the chair by the window.

"I don't remember inviting you into my room," Storm sighed, dropping his right hand to his side. He wondered if King had any idea how close had come to being dead. Then Storm decided that King probably did. The guy was sharp.

"You didn't. I invited myself in," King gave him a crooked smile.

"I knew that already," Storm told him.

"So, what did you find?" King asked.

"Sorenson was definitely taken. I'm pretty sure that Bergdorf knows by who. I saw it on the video feed, but didn't mention it to Bergdorf. The guy gave me a bad feeling," Storm replied.

"I'll have my people do a deep dive on the guy. If he is dirty, we will find it," King replied.

"Do that, and let me know."

"Roger that."

"Anything else?"

"Just watch your back. I'll be in touch," King stood and left the room. Storm gave him five minutes before turning on the radio to cover his actions. Storm opened the hidden compartment in his suitcase and removed his bug detector and swept the room. King had left three devices behind. Storm flushed them all down the toilet. He was beginning to trust his Company contact even less.

Using an encryption program on his phone, Storm placed a call to Larry Dixon back in Key West. "Sorenson was taken. I sent you a video clip showing what happened. Can you check it out and see if there is anything to help identify the kidnappers?" Storm asked when Dixon picked up.

"Yeah, I got it and I'll do what I can. Why aren't you on the laptop?" Dixon asked.

"Because Jim King was in my room when I got back. He left three listening devices behind," Storm replied.

"Turn your laptop on and open it. I can check and see if he put a keystroke logger or any other kind of malware on it. Smart thinking to use your phone," Dixon told him.

"Well, I have been doing this shit for a while now. Now, I just need to figure out what to do next," Storm said before he broke the connection. After hanging up, he opened his laptop and booted it up so that Dixon could check it out remotely.

Storm realized that he was hungry. He left his room and headed downstairs. He headed for Pelón. It had a 4.4-star rating and from what the desk clerk had told him featured an awesome menu for international travelers.

Storm took a taxi from his hotel to the restaurant. He had kept an eye out for any surveillance that might be watching him. So far, it appeared, he was clean. Nick knew that couldn't last. The people who had kidnapped Sorenson would be aware by now that Storm was looking for the missing scientist. The question was what would they do about it?

Some sort of lethal force, most likely. He would just have to be ready for it. By the time Nick had finished his meal it was after sundown. It was quiet when he walked outside, his senses went on high alert. One thing he knew about Limon was that it had the most crime per capita in the country.

If there was going to be trouble, it would likely be while he was on the way back to his hotel. That was something he could handle, something that he could fight. Storm smiled as he dialed a number for the local taxi service. It didn't take long for one of the taxis to arrive. Nick stepped inside and gave the driver the address of his hotel. The vehicle pulled away from the curb and into traffic.

~ ~ ~

Arturo Diaz stood in the camp and waited for the Boss to summon him into the commander's tent. Diaz was not happy about the news that he was about to deliver. He knew instinctively that the Boss would not be happy about it either.

The prisoner made Diaz nervous, but the mercenary tried to ignore that. He was uncomfortable about dealing with killer germs that he couldn't even see. Major Parker stepped out the door of the tent and waved him inside. As if the well-muscled Major with his shaved skull and dark blue eyes wasn't intimidating enough, his Boss was even more frightening.

Dante Schultz was also a big man and looked fit enough to wrestle a Polar bear. Like parker, his skull was shaved. But a long scar bisected his face from left to right. His left eye was white and blind. His khaki t-shirt stretched across his massive chest. "Report," Schultz commanded.

"The man from the CDC arrived to check out the lab. Bergdorf didn't think he found anything, but Bergdorf is an idiot. This man, Nathan Simms, is going to be a problem," Diaz explained.

"You seem sure of this," Schultz observed.

"I am. I have watched this man. He doesn't move like a scientist. He moves more like a spy," Diaz replied.

"Pick a team and take this man. I want to know who he really is," Schultz commanded.

"Copy that," Diaz replied, snapping off a salute and spinning on his heel to exit the tent. Schultz watched him go with a frown.

"Follow him and be prepared if he runs into problems. This Simms seems to be more of a problem than what Arturo thinks," Schultz told Parker.

"Copy that, Boss," Parker replied before heading out of the tent. Dante Schultz leaned back in his chair. He had taken this job and he planned to see it through. Adrian Kurieg had hired him to kidnap Tristan Sorenson. Schultz still wasn't sure why.

~ ~ ~

Nick Storm arrived safely back at his hotel. He headed up to his room after purchasing a couple of bottled waters and some chips before heading to his room. Nick had played his part to perfection. He was sure that whoever was behind Sorenson's kidnapping that would be coming for him, or rather Nathan Simms.

Nick kicked off his shoes and slipped his pistol out of his pocket holster and put it on the desk beside his lap top. Nick opened one of the bottles of water and the bag of chips before he opened the laptop and booted it back up. He was hoping that there might be word from Dixon or King via e-mail in the time that he had been gone.

Storm typed in Tristan Sorenson's name in the search bar for Google. It would give him whatever there was to be known publicly about the scientist. He would do a deep dive on the guy in government databases later.

Tristan Sorenson had earned his degree in Microbiology and Virology at Stanford University. He was 35 years old unmarried. Sorenson stood six-feet tall with curly brown hair and blue eyes. He had graduated at the top of his class and had gone right away into government service. Once he had entered government service, Tristan Sorenson had virtually dropped off the face of the earth.

Nick leaned back in his chair. That was a red flag. It meant that somebody in the U.S. Government was bankrolling his research. That was *not* good news. Nick opened up his e-mail and composed a quick letter to Jack Riley, giving him an update on everything that had happened so far.

Once that was done, he ordered a bottle of vodka and cranberry juice from room service. Once it had arrived, Nick made himself a drink and watched some of the local television. Before long, Storm was asleep.

~ ~ ~

Tristan Sorenson struggled against the ropes that bound him to the chair. The hemp rope was digging into his skin, tearing it and soon he could feel blood running down his wrists to his hands. Sorenson had no idea who these men were that had kidnapped him. He didn't even know if he was still in Limon. Sorenson was beginning to wish he had never taken this government job. He had no idea that it would be so dangerous.

He had been shocked when the masked men with guns had burst into his lab and killed his assistant. Gina had not deserved that. They had tied his hands behind his back, gathered up his research files and dragged him out of the lab. They had forced him into a dark-colored SUV and then put a bag over his head so that he couldn't see where they were going.

Sorenson didn't know how long that they had travelled but he was pretty sure that it had been at least a few hours. He didn't know for sure, but he had a fair idea of why he had been taken. It had to be about Valhalla. Sorenson closed his eyes and exhaled a long- drawn-out breath.

He shook his head, wishing that he had never engineered the super-virus. Should Valhalla be released in the world, it would wipe out most of the life on earth, human and animal. He cursed himself for following the research that created the virus. It was too late now. Now, what he needed to do was find a way the neutralize the virus before his captors could develop a delivery system to spread it across the face of the Earth.

Tristan closed his eyes and tried to relax. He needed his rest so that he would be sharp enough to screw up his captor's plans. Soon, he was asleep.

~ ~ ~

Arturo Diaz had spent hours on the telephone. But it had proven worthwhile. He had a location on Nathan Simms. He would take Diego and Pablo with him and they would eliminate the man from the American CDC. He snapped an order at the two and they rose and followed him out the door.

Arturo took the driver's seat and he started the engine as the other two climbed into the car. Both men carried sub-machine guns. Arturo grinned as he put the car in gear. Nathan Simms would die tonight.

Nick awakened from a sound sleep fully awake. His right hand found the grip of his pistol as he rolled off the bed. Nick slowed his breathing and listened for any sound that might have awakened him.

Over the years working as an intelligence agent, he had developed a sixth sense for danger. Trouble was coming his way. He heard the elevator ding as it had arrived on his floor. Then footsteps approaching his room. There were two, no three men from the sound of their footsteps as they drew closer.

The locks were electric and needed a key card to unlock them. The dead bolt was also set, but Nick was pretty sure that it wouldn't survive automatic weapons fire. So, he had to be ready to react when they crashed into his room.

Gunshots blew the deadbolt off the door. Nick grinned as he thumbed the safety off on his pistol and aimed at the door. Someone kicked it in and Storm fired, the bullet catching the front man and driving him back. Nick ducked as auto-fire ripped into the bed beside him. He slithered to the end of the bed and blew the head off the second man through the door. The third man turned and ran. Nick was on his feet and running for the door. He swung out in to the hall as the man reached the elevator. Nick fired and dropped the man before the doors opened. People were coming out of their rooms as Nick reached the elevators and kicked the man's gun away.

People were staring at him and the pistol he had. So much for his legend. It looked like the cat was out of the bag now. Storm headed back to his room. He figured the cops were on the way and he needed to get a safety net in place. Once in his room, he grabbed his phone and called Jack Riley back in the Keys. Caribe may have officially disbanded, but Riley still had connections in the intelligence circles and might be able to keep him out of a Costa Rican jail. At least, Nick hoped so.

If not for having been seen by so many people, Nick would have just packed his bag and slipped away. However, since he had been seen by so many people that was no longer an option. He could hear the sirens approaching and voices were growing louder in the hall. He snatched the dead man's pistol and hid his own. Both were 9mm so there was a good chance that the cops might buy it. For now, it was the best he could do. He put the dead man's pistol on the desk, just out of his reach even should he be tempted to lunge for it. He hoped that the cops would appreciate that and not just shoot him like a rabid dog as they came through the door.

A man in police uniform stepped through the door, his hand on the but of his pistol. The policeman swept the room with his eyes, taking in the bullet shredded door, the position of the dead man in the room. "You are Nathan Simms?" the officer inquired.

"I am. I work for the Center for Disease Control in the United States. I am down here looking into the disappearance of Dr. Tristan Sorenson from Microbe LLC. These men broke into my room and tried to kill me," Storm replied.

"They certainly did not succeed. Where did a medical professional learn to do this?" the officer asked, waving g at the dead bodies.

"I wasn't always a scientist or investigator. I served in the United States Marine Corps," Nick replied.

"I am Sergeant Angelo Diego, of the Limon police department. Do you have your papers?"

"I do," Nick replied. He grabbed the papers and ID that Jim King had given him. Nick hoped that they were good enough to undergo the close scrutiny of the local cops. He figured they were, but was still a little nervous. He still didn't trust King, and he suspected this would be the litmus test that he said he was on the level or that he wasn't

Five

The first person through the door was wearing a municipal police uniform. Nick sat calmly and quietly as more people arrived. Finally, a guy in a rumpled suit arrived. Storm figured him to be a detective of some kind.

"Mister Simms?" the man asked.

"Yes," Nick replied. He had taken the time to memorize his legend so if he found himself in this situation, he could make it believable.

"May I take possession of the firearm on the desk?"

"You may. What is your name?"

"I am Sergeant Jose Lopez. Are you responsible for all of this?" Lopez waved at the dead bodies.

"I am. They broke into my room and we struggled, I got the gun away and fought for my life," Nick explained.

"You seem to have vigorously defended yourself, Mr. Simms," Lopez observed.

"I did," Nick agreed.

"How were you able to do all of this? I am sure that it was not covered in CDC training."

"It was not. Before I joined the CDC, I was a Force Recon Marine," Nick replied. That part of his legend was actually true.

"This is some sort of special forces?" Lopez asked.

"Yes, it is. We are the elite of the Marine Corps," Nick explained.

"So, I understand that you are saying that you were attacked and then took out three men? That would be a correct account of what happened?" Lopez asked.

"It would," Nick replied.

"Interesting," Lopez murmured.

"Not really," Nick shook his head.

"You are not to leave the country without informing me first. I may have further questions for you."

"Sure thing, Sergeant Lopez," Nick smiled.

The Sergeant gave him a questioning look before turning and leaving the room. He took the gun from the desk as well. Nick smiled as he watched him go. Sergeant Lopez was no fool. He just had nothing to counter the story that Nick had told him. But Nick could tell that the guy was a bulldog

Lopez would worry this like a dog with a bone. That would make him a problem if Nick had to leave town to follow the people that had taken Tristan Sorenson. That meant that Nick would have to work harder to find the man before his captors moved him out of Limon.

Storm called the front desk and asked to be moved to a different room. A few moments later the hotel had sent someone to move him to a different room. This time one on the ground floor. He had insisted on that. The ground floor gave him better access to escape routes than the second floor had.

Being able to slip away from violence was much better than confronting it. Escaping meant that there would be less police involvement than when there were dead bodies all over the place, as tonight had proven.

Nick opened his computer and dialed Riley for an encrypted Zoom call. Riley came on-line within seconds. "Hey Nick, what can I do for you?" Riley asked.

"Find me what you can on a Sergeant Jose Lopez from the Limon Civil Police. He is investigating the attack on my hotel room," Nick explained.

"I'll do what I can. You watch your back," Riley admonished him.

"Copy that, Boss," Nick replied, ending the call. Storm grinned, knowing that Riley hated being called Boss. Especially since his organization had officially disbanded. Still, it felt right. He didn't trust Jim King or the CIA. So, as far Storm was concerned this was just a single operative mission for Caribe.

Storm opened his secure browser and started seeing what he could find out about Bergdorf and Microbe LLC. As it turned out, Microbe LLC was based out of Germany. That was interesting. Why would a German company specializing in microbiology and finding cures for virus' be sponsoring a lab in a third world country like Costa Rica? Yet another question that he needed answers to.

~ ~ ~

Sergeant Jose Lopez frowned as he drove his car back to the local police station. The American had not been entirely truthful with him. Lopez was sure of it. The man from the CDC was hiding something. Once he had arrived in his office, Lopez booted his computer and started a search for Nathan Simms of the Center for Disease Control.

It didn't take him long to pull up a complete file on Nathan Simms as well as a photo. It was the same man. Lopez frowned. The man appeared to be legitimate. So, why were his instincts telling him that the man was lying?

~ ~ ~

Jim King frowned. None of the bugs that he planted in Storm's room were working. That was odd to say the least. Unless Storm had scanned for listening devices. Of course, he did. Nick Storm had never been the trusting type, not even back in his CIA days. King shook his head. He should have expected it. However, it just made him surer that he had recruited the right man for the job.

Storm was an experienced operative, one of the best, if not the best, that he had ever met. King had worked with him before across the pond in both Europe and Africa. They had butted heads on a couple of missions, but they had achieved their objectives. That's why he had selected Storm for this particular mission. He had faith that Storm could find Sorenson and recover or destroy his research before it fell into the wrong hands.

~ ~ ~

Nick slipped out of the hotel after sunset. He had managed to find the addresses of a couple of people who also worked at Microbe LLC with Dr. Sorenson. He was hoping that they might be able to give him some answers. Since Dr. Bergdorf had tried to stonewall him. Nick figured that Bergdorf had to be a part of whatever had happened to Sorenson. If he couldn't get any information from Sorenson's co-workers, he would revisit Bergdorf. The second visit would not be as polite as the first one.

Storm was armed this time out because he planned on avoiding any run-ins with the local police. They were just regular guys trying to make a living. But if he ran into any of the guys that had taken Sorenson, well, it was open season on them.

~ ~ ~

The Sunset Mango sounded like a place that nerdy scientists would go to blow off steam and pretend that they were not just science nerd. Nick had called a cab and it arrived within ten minutes, something that would normally be considered a record in Limon. The cabbie tried talking but Nick ignored him until the man finally gave up.

The Sunset Mango was in a seedier part of Limon, but Nick didn't let that bother him. It was no worse than Venezuela. He had been there on one of his early missions as part of Caribe. Or another European third world country he had been sent to by the CIA.

The inside of the bar was dark wood paneling and low lights. Smoke clouds were moved by ceiling fans and air-conditioning. A large Black man worked behind the bar, his head shaved and gleaming in the low light. Large yellowish eyes caught sight of Storm as he entered the bar and watched him as he approached the bar.

"Beer," Nick told him. He didn't want anything stronger because he needed to keep his wits about him. This probe was dangerous because he was not that familiar with the territory. That meant he had to remain on full alert to make sure he didn't end up dead.

The bartender sat a bottle of beer in front of him and then moved away to take care of customers on the other end of the bar. A calypso band was playing on stage as Nick took a drink from his beer and turned on the bar stool so that he could take a look at the other patrons of the bar.

They were an ugly bunch for the most part. Except for a corner table in the back. The people sitting at that table were more like frightened rabbits surrounded by wolves. Those had to be the people from the lab. Storm took his bottle of beer and headed over to the table of lab rats.

When he reached the table, he spun a chair around and dropped into it. Putting his arms on the back as he studied the group. They stared at him with frightened eyes. Nick sighed. This was not going to be easy. Somehow, Nick had to win them over and get them to talk.

Hey, I'm Nathan Simms from the Center for Disease Control. Do y'all work at Microbe LLC?" he asked.

"Yeah, we do," replied one of the men. He was thin and looked more like a skeleton than a man.

"You are?" Nick asked.

"Stanley Logston. I am a project manager at Microbe," the man said.

"What can you tell me about Tristan Sorenson?" Nick asked.

"Houdini himself," the man frowned, shaking his head.

"You are?"

"Ted Foster. I was working on another project until the incredible vanishing scientist Tristan Sorenson arrived. Then he got all of the new equipment and lab techs, draining needed resources from the rest of us," Foster replied.

"He's a damn diva is what he is," snarled an older man with a full white beard.

"You're just pissed because he stole away Gina out of your lab and into his project, James," Foster scoffed.

"Then he just disappeared, along with all of his research," added a timid-looking young man who seemed to be trying and failing to grow a beard. To Nick he looked like he was barely 21 years old, if that.

"You are pissed because Gina Torres also blew you off to work with Sorenson," Foster chuckled.

"You are?" Nick looked at the kid expectantly.

"Mark Ross," the kid replied, taking a pull on his beer.

"Who is this Gina Torres you mentioned?" It was a name Nick hadn't heard until now.

"Gina is a brilliant young research assistant. Until she became enthralled by Sorenson and his Valhalla project," James Mercer interjected.

"So, what happened to her?" Nick asked.

"Gina disappeared the day after Sorenson. She came in the day he disappeared and was suddenly really nervous," Ross explained.

"What do you think made her so nervous?"

"Maybe the sudden way that Sorenson was just gone, along with all of his research materials," Ross shrugged. Nick studied the young man's face. The kid had it bad for this Gina Torres. Why hadn't Stromberg mentioned that she had left suddenly too? This was getting stranger by the minute.

"Shit, we gotta get out of here," Ted Foster said suddenly, his face suddenly pale in the poor light. Mercer and Ross scooted their chairs back as well.

"What's wrong?" Nick asked, looking over his shoulder. Three men in military fatigues had entered the bar. Nick turned and the three scientists were gone, vanishing as quickly as any stage magician. Nick stood and turned sliding his chair back around and sliding it up to the table. The three men were heading his way. That couldn't be good.

Nick took a pull of his beer, nearly emptying the bottle. He waited as the men closed in on him. They looked like tough guys, likely muscle for somebody that didn't want the man from the CDC asking too many questions about Tristin Sorenson. One of the men stopped in front of him while the other two spread out a yard or so behind the lead man to the left and right. They seemed to figure that they had him boxed in. Nick smiled.

"Hola," Nick said, eyeing the three of them and tried to look scared.

"You shouldn't be here," the leader told him in thickly accented English.

"Why not?" Nick asked putting a confused look on his face. In his head he was already planning his attack, who was first, which one would be second and how to take down the third before he headed for the door. The rest of the cliental might jump in to help the three, but Nick hoped that they wouldn't. He had his gun, but he really didn't want to use it if that could be avoided.

The leader stepped forward, telegraphing his punch, except Nick wasn't there when it landed. He had side stepped and swung the partial bottle of beer and shattered it across the man's face. Sharp edges of glass tore at the guy's skin as beer and blood sprayed into his eyes. The leader fell back with a scream of pain as Nick snapped out a side kick into the one of the right's guts momentarily burying his booted foot there, pulling his foot back and delivering a back-fist punch into the throat of the guy on the left, sending him staggering back into a table full of people.

The leader was charging again after wiping the beer and blood from his eyes. Nick feinted a kick and drove his fist into the point of the man's chin, putting the guy down for the count. A chair snapped past Storm's face, swung by the guy on the right, his face flushed red with rage. Nick stepped back and hooked a chair with his right foot and kicked it up at the remaining combatant. The chairs collided with a crash and shattered.

Storm rushed forward and delivered a kick to the man's groin that would probably hit a fifty-yard field goal and then kept moving on past him until he was out the door. Nick rushed away towards the waterfront, figuring that it might be the easiest place to get lost. Those men had not attacked him by accident. The way the three guys from the lab had vanished made that clear enough.

The trio had recognized the men that had attacked him. Nick wanted to find out where from. He suspected that they might have been part of the security team for Microbe LLC, but he couldn't really prove it. For the moment, he just wanted to get out of sight until things cooled down. He could hear the bleating of the klaxon horns of the city police in the distance behind him.

Nick was more than willing to bet that he could expect another visit from Sergeant Lopez bright and early. For the moment, he put distance between himself and the Sunset Mango and hoped that nobody in the bar had gotten a good look at him. At least not well enough to give a decent description.

Six

Nick was back in his room by two o'clock in the morning. He still had no real answers to the questions about what had befallen Dr. Sorenson. Other that the man and his research had been taken by force. Whatever was going on, it was clear that Stromberg was a party to it. Had Stromberg sold Sorenson out? It appeared likely.

For the moment, Nick had far more questions than he did answers. He stripped off his clothes after securing the door to his room. He slipped his pistol under his pillow within easy reach, closed his eyes and quickly fell asleep.

~ ~ ~

Gina Torres had abandoned her apartment in the city. Tristan had warned her that something might happen to him and said if it did, she should run. He had refused to say why. Gina was a Latinx beauty, with bronzed skin and reddish-brown hair. Her eyes were a dark brown. Most men found her attractive. She had known this from a young age.

Tristan had been afraid that something was going to happen. He had been right. Of course, Stromberg denied any knowledge of anything other than Dr. Sorenson had vanished along with all of his work.

He had told Gina the day before he had vanished that he had made a break through and it frightened him. It frightened him because he had realized that his discovery could be turned into a deadly biological weapon. That was not something that he wanted any part of. But someone had found out.

Gina wanted to find Tristan. She had admitted to herself it was for selfish reasons. She had fallen for the scientist as they had worked together in the lab. Long hours and constant contact had stirred the chemistry between them. Late one night, alone in the lab, they had acted on it. They had been lovers ever since. Then two days ago, Tristan had vanished as if he had never been. She had expected to see him when she reported to work yesterday, but he was gone and the lab was empty, stripped of computers and paper files. Almost as if it had never been there to begin with.

Gina shuddered at the thought. Who could make someone disappear so thoroughly? Tristan had told her that much of his funding had come from the United States government. Were they behind his disappearance? It was possible. Gina had stayed away from work and fled her small apartment. Currently, she was staying with a friend that she had grown up with. The telephone rang, the sudden sound causing Gina to jump. She reached for it. "Hello?"

"Gina?" asked a familiar voice.

"Stan?" Gina recognized Stanly Logston, the project manager at the lab. "How did you find me?"

"That's not important. There is a guy claiming to be from the CDC back in the States asking a lot of questions about Tristan and his work. He may come looking for you."

"Why would he do that?" Gina asked.

"I don't know, but it probably has something to do with Tristan's research. I don't trust this guy. You shouldn't either. He may actually be here to tie up loose ends," Stan told her.

"Does this guy have a name?"

"The guy said his name was Nathan Simms, but I don't believe him. Keep your head down and avoid him if you can," Stan told her before breaking the connection. It took a moment for her to remember that Stan had not told her how he had found her. That set off alarm bells in her head. Gina grabbed her over-size purse which had extra clothes, her wallet and credit cards and her cell phone in it. She grabbed her keys and ran for the door. She had a bad feeling that she needed to get gone from her friend's apartment as quickly as possible.

~ ~ ~

Arturo Diaz and his team were on their way to the girl's location. Logston had given it to them by getting Gina Torres on the phone so they could trace the call. Having the project manager working for them had garnered far more fruit than Bergdorf, the manager of the lab facility. It didn't take long to reach the building where the girl had been hiding. Diaz parked the car and he and his men got out, heading for the building. Gina Torres was as good as dead.

~ ~ ~

Nick was already up and dressed when the expected knock came on his door. He took a quick glance through the peep hole in the door. As expected, Sergeant Lopez stood on the other side. Nick removed the dead bolt and opened the door. "Good morning, Sergeant."

"*Buenos Dias*, Senior Simms. Did you rest well last night?"

"I did. Would you like a cup of coffee? The coffee maker here in the room makes up to four cups, and I'm on my first," Nick offered.

"No thank you, Senior Simms. We had some excitement in town last night. A particularly lethal bar fight. Did you hear anything about that?"

"Not until right now. After my supper, I went to bed and slept like a baby."

"I hope you are not, as you Yankees like to say, holding out on me."

"Why would I?"

"Because too many dead bodies have turned up in my city since this Dr. Sorenson went missing. It hurts tourism. And that makes me very upset, because tourism is important to my country."

"I understand, Sergeant. I should be able to wrap things up after I visit the lab today. Once I am done there, I'll head back to San Juan to catch a flight back to the States," Nick replied.

"See that you do Senior Simms. I will be keeping an eye on you. Have a good day," Lopez said before turning and walking out. Nick knew that he had been fortunate that Lopez had not posted guards outside his door last night. He had a feeling he wouldn't be that lucky tonight.

Nick poured another cup of coffee when another knock sounded and his door opened. Jim King entered his room uninvited yet once again. "What did you do to get the local cops on your ass?"

"Good morning to you as well. Three guys tried to take me out here at the hotel yesterday. I had to defend myself."

"You're lucky you're not sitting in a Costa Rican jail cell."

"Fortunately, I had plenty of witnesses that it was self-defense."

"Good thing. Anyway, have you found anything new about Sorenson?" King asked.

"He was involved with a lab assistant."

"Involved? You mean sexually?"

"Yes. Her name is Gina Torres and she is nearly as brilliant as our missing scientist, according to her co-workers at Microbe. I think she might be worth looking into," Nick said.

"Fine, I'll put some people on finding her. So, what's your next move?" King asked.

"I'm heading back to the lab to interview some of Sorenson's colleagues to see what I can learn from them about him." Nick didn't mention that he had met some of them the night before. As far as he was concerned, King didn't need to know that.

"Okay, keep me in the loop," King said, heading for the door. Nick watched his CIA handler go and was happier for it. King hadn't gotten the chance to plant anymore bugs this time around. Not yet anyway.

Nick prepared for his trip out to the lab. He called for a taxi before heading down stairs to the lobby to wait for it. He was hoping a surprise visit at the lab today would shake up the four men that he had spoken with last night. He also wanted to learn more about Gina Torres and what she might know about Sorenson's work on Valhalla.

~ ~ ~

Wilhelm Stromberg was not happy to see Nick walking once more in to the lobby of the building that housed the lab complex. His eyes widened and his face paled under his tan. "Mister Simms, why are you back here?"

"I want to speak with Dr. Sorenson's co-workers as well as others who work in the lab. It might help shed light on Sorenson's disappearance," Nick replied. He glanced at his watch. "Time is important. I'd like to speak to the project manager first. His name, I believe, is Stanley Logston?"

"Ah, give me a moment to see if Mr. Logston is available," Stromberg sighed, moving to a desk in the lobby. He picked up a phone and dialed a number inside the building. "Mr. Logston, there is a man in the lobby to see you. I suggest you meet with him forthwith," Stromberg said. He listened for a few beats. "I'll send him to your office." Stromberg looked at Nick. "Take the elevator to the second floor. Logston's office is the second door on the left."

"Thank you," Nick replied, heading for the bank of elevators that stood head of him. Nick watched Stromberg in one of the security mirrors as the man picked the phone up and dialed another number. The elevator arrived and Nick stepped inside and pressed the button for the second floor. The doors of the elevator slid closed and then it was lifting up to the next floor.

The elevator doors opened into a brightly lit corridor with dark blue carpeting. Nick stepped out into the corridor and turned left. He moved silently down the corridor to the second door on the left. Nick knocked twice and opened the door and stepped inside.

"I'll be with you in a minute," Logston said, not looking up from the papers on his desk.

"Take your time, Stanley. I've got plenty of it," Nick said quietly. Logston's head jerked up in surprise.

"You!"

"Yes, Stan, it is me," Nick replied.

"How are you here?" Logston asked.

"You mean how did I evade those leg-breakers that you sicced on me? Violently. What I want you to do now is tell me why?" Nick replied, moving deeper into the office.

"Listen, I don't know what you're talking about Simms. I sent nobody after you."

"That's yet another lie you've told me, Stan. I'm starting to think you don't like me. It hurts, because I've been told I'm a very likeable guy."

"I'm a busy man, Simms. I don't have time for your foolishness. Get out before I can security!" Nick had enough. He reached across the desk and grabbed Logston by the lapels of his lab coat and dragged him across the desk.

"I've had enough of your bullshit, Stan. Who took Sorenson and his research? We both know he was taken by force. By the way, you're not as good at texting as you might think. That's how I know that you called in the leg-breakers last night at the Sunset Mango. One more chance. Who took Sorenson?" Nick demanded.

"They were mercenaries. The work for a guy named Parker. He calls himself a Major. That's all I know," Stan gasped out the words.

"Where can I find this Major Parker and his people?"

"They were taking Sorenson north, maybe Nicaragua, that's all I know." Logston said. Nick tossed him back across the desk into his chair. A bullet blaster a hole through the window sending glass flying before blasting through Logston's head.

Nick dropped to the floor drawing his Ruger SC9 and thumbing off the safety. Three more shots exploded through the glass, sending fragments flying. The desk sheltered Nick from most of them. This was going to be a problem. Nick crawled to Logston's office trashcan. It was full of discarded papers. Excellent! Nick pulled out a disposable lighter and set fire to the papers. Once they were burning good, he kicked the can over and dropped the burning paper on the carpet which caught fire quickly. Smoke billowed up and filled the room. Keeping low, Storm sprinted for the door. More rifle shots followed him out.

Once in the corridor, nick dived to the right and rolled up into a combat crouch, his pistol extended out in front of him. He moved towards the elevator and saw it had been called down to the first floor. Uh-oh. More trouble on the way. Nick stood up and ran toward the stairwell at the end of the corridor. He was just passing through the fire door when he heard the elevator arrive. Glancing back through the small glass window and saw four men in military garb rush out with their weapons levelled in breeching position. Shit! Nick headed up the stairs, figuring more men would be coming up the stairs behind him.

The lab complex was only four stories tall and the fire alarm and sprinkler system had already been tripped. Still, smoke was billowing up from the second floor so Nick doubted the efficiency of the sprinkler system.

The fourth floor was empty, none of the labs being in actual use. Still, there were chemicals and equipment that Nick could use. It only took a couple of moments to pour mineral oil on both of the fourth-floor landings. The excess oil ran down the steps making them slippery as well. Storm placed a quick call from his iPhone and then spilled chemicals that if ignited would produce a heavy gas that would burn the sinus and eyes of the mercs that were after him. Once he fired it, he needed to get on the roof.

Nick smashed out a window and made an expedient grappling hook out of angle iron and fire hose. He leaned out the window and tossed the hook to the roof. It caught. Nick stepped onto the window sill as bullets ripped through the corridor. Nick dropped a burning match to the chemical-soaked carpet which ignited immediately. Nick stepped out and began to climb his make-shift rope to the roof.

Nick had just rolled over the roof ledge when a bullet chipped the bricks near his face. Rolling behind part of the HVAC system, Storm drew his pistol once more, searching for the deadly enemy that had thought he might head for the roof.

Bullets punched through the thin metal and sent him scrambling for better cover. Storm rounded a corner and spotted the shooter. He fired, sending the other man diving for cover. Heat and smoke were pouring out of the building as the fire inside became more than the sprinklers could handle. Nick crouched and ran closer to where the other man was hiding. The man popped up and they fired at the same time. The other man missed, but Nick did not.

Suddenly, the whup-whup of helicopter rotary blades became audible.

The pilot swooped down and hovered just above the roof. Nick ran and jumped inside and the chopper lifted up and away from the burning lab complex. Nick holstered his pistol and climbed into the co-pilot's seat of the Vietnam era Huey Cobra. "You called for a taxi?" Jay Barr asked him.

"I did," Nick replied with a cough. Some of the smoke had gotten into his lungs.

Seven

Nick wasn't overly surprised to see Jay Barr piloting the helicopter. The pilot worked on a "per job" basis for Caribe. Nick had no doubt that Jack had put him on standby just in case Storm needed a quick extraction. "Thanks for the pick-up," Nick told him.

"I was in the neighborhood. Where do you want to go?" Barr asked.

"Can you make it to San Juan?"

"I can with fuel to spare."

"Then take me to San Juan. I'll contact Jack when I get there."

"You're in charge," Barr shrugged heading for the capital.

~ ~ ~

Gina Torres was running scared. She had witnessed armed men busting into her friend's apartment. She had taken her car and had headed north. She could get lost in San Juan. It was a much bigger place that Limon.

Tristan had told her that he had stashed several thumb drives with copies of all of his research in San Jose. If she could find those drives, she might be able to trade them for Tristan. Or it might get her killed. Either way, she had to try.

It would take her just under three hours to make the 155-kilometer drive to San Juan. With luck, she would come up with a plan by the time she got there. Gina kept an eye on her mirrors, looking for any vehicles that might not be regular traffic. Somebody was willing to kill to keep Valhalla a secret. She didn't want to be the next victim.

~ ~ ~

Arturo Diaz was furious! The girl was gone by the time they got into the apartment where she had been staying. He was sure that they hadn't missed her by much, but the men he had sent to scour the neighborhood had come up empty. Where could she have gone? Major Parker would not be happy, nor would Dante Schultz. Diaz swallowed hard. He had seen what happened to people who displeased Dante Schultz.

Most were dead. With a heartfelt sigh, Diaz commanded his men to return to the cars. They would head back to the compound. Muttering a curse, Diaz activated and dropped an incendiary device on the carpeted floor and shut and locked the door behind him. As the three cars sped out of town and back to the base, windows exploded from the apartment and flames climbed up the side of the building.

~ ~ ~

Sergeant Jose Lopez frowned as he stared at the still smoking ruins of the Microbe LLC building. His first thought was that Nathan Simms had something to do with this. There was something about the man that he just didn't trust. Lopez had a thing about people who lied to him. He didn't like it. And he was certain that Nathan Simms of the CDC was not exactly who he claimed to be. It was time to have another talk with the man. Lopez climbed into his police car and headed back into Limon.

~ ~ ~

San Juan, Costa Rica.

Nick took a taxi from the airport back to his hotel. Once there, he quickly packed his things. It was time that he found a new base of operations away from where Sgt. Lopez could find him. The Nathan

Simms legend was now a liability. Fortunately, Nick had prepared for this. He took new identification and credit cards from the hidden compartment in his suitcase. And placed the Nathan Simms credentials back in the compartment and sealed it again. Once everything was packed, he left via the back door and walked six blocks before calling for another taxi, on that would take him to the northern part of the city.

Chayote Lodge was 4.9 miles out of San Jose. The Lodge was located in Zarcero and had a restaurant, a concierge service, bar, garden and terrace. Both WIFI and private parking were available at the lodge free of charge. Nick checked under the name of Noah Stark. Hopefully, he was far enough from Limon that he wouldn't have to worry about Sgt. Lopez. The man was a bulldog. Nick had seen that with his own eyes.

Lopez had doubted him from the beginning, but there had been nothing that Nick could have done to prevent that. Luckily, Riley had sent someone to San Jose airport to fly out of the country as Nathan Simms of the CDC. Nick wondered how big a shit fit that Jim King was going to throw when Nick contacted him. He suspected it would be a big one. Oh well, fuck him if he couldn't take a joke.

Nick pulled out his laptop and turned it on. He connected to the hotel WIFI system and opened an encrypted zoom call to Key West. Larry Dixon came on in seconds. "I see you got out of the lab complex," Dixon commented.

"Thanks to Jack and Jay Barr," Nick acknowledged.

"Did you find out anything helpful?" Jack Riley asked as he joined the call.

"Maybe. I'm pretty sure that the project manager and the facility manager were both in on the kidnapping," Nick explained.

"So, Sorenson was set up from the beginning," Riley concluded.

"It looks that way. Can you find out what agency Sorenson was working for?"

"I'll see what I can find. I may have been forced into early retirement, but I still have people that owe me in Foggy Bottom," Riley told him.

"Do what you can. I'll see what I can find out here in San Jose," Nick replied.

"Copy that," Dixon and Riley said and then the connection was severed. Nick had an idea of where to start looking. Dominic Garada was head of the largest crime family in San Jose. He would know if someone was encroaching on his territory. He also owed Nick a few favors from the old days. Now it was time for Nick to call those favors in. Nick pulled out his cell phone and dialed Garda from memory. Then he settled in and waited for the call to connect. It started to ring on the other end. It rang once, twice, and then a third time before a familiar voice answered.

"Hello?" the voice asked.

"Dominic? This is Nick Storm. I need a favor," Nick told him.

~ ~ ~

Gina Torres drove to San Jose. She felt safer being out of Limon and far away from the lab. But where to go? That was the question. But what was the answer? So far, she didn't have one. However, Tristan had given her a name and a number in San Juan, somebody to contact if something happened to him. Gina had never thought that she would need to use it. But now she needed to. She pulled up to a curb next to a pay phone.

Gina glanced around, checking to see if anybody seemed to be watching her. Nobody was. She stepped into the telephone booth and dropped a few coins in the slot and dialed the number from memory. "Yes?" a man's voice answered.

"Something has happened to Tristan. People are after me. He said you could help," Gina explained.

"Okay. How long can you stay at this number?" the voice asked.

"A few minutes, but no more. I don't know how far behind me they are."

"I'll call you back in two minutes," the voice said before the connection was severed. Gina frowned. She felt exposed out on the street like this with just a thin plexiglass pane between her and any potential bullets.

Gina glanced at her watch. She was watching the clock. When it hit two minutes, she was gone. She couldn't afford to stay any longer than that. Not when people were after her to kill her. Gina waited. At one minute and fifty-five seconds, the telephone rang. Gina snatched it up. "Yes?"

"Go to the Government building. A man will meet you there. He's very capable and will protect you. He also wants to find Dr. Sorenson," the voice told her.

"Does he have a name?" Gina asked.

"He does. Noah Stark. Watch for him," Jim King told her.

~ ~ ~

Nick was surprised when his cellphone rang. It was Jim King. Nick answered.

"Sorenson's lady just called. She will meet you at the San Juan government building within the hour. Get there before the bad guys do," King told him.

"Copy that," Nick replied before hanging up. King had not seemed surprised that Nick was not still in Limon, and now he was sending him a woman to protect while he was still hunting for Sorenson. King knew more than what he had shared with Nick. Storm was certain of that. The next time he saw King, the man was going to give him a few answers to his questions about what was really going on!

~ ~ ~

Jim King frowned as he hung up the phone. Things were starting to happen too fast. First Sorenson's vanishing act, the attempts on Storm when he had barely started investigating, the lab in Limon being burnt to the ground and now Gina Torres showing up in San Juan and needing protection. The whole operation was starting to turn into one giant clusterfuck!

The fact that somebody had taken the bait of Tristan Sorenson's work and kidnapped the guy meant that somebody believed what Sorenson had been selling. Somebody that wanted a superbug that could be weaponized as a weapon of mass destruction. The question was who? That was what Jim King needed to know. Hopefully Nick Storm could find the answer.

Tristan Sorenson sagged against the wall of the ramshackle hut. The jungle air was thick and did its best to suck every drop of moisture out of his aching body. He didn't know who the men were that had kidnapped him, but he knew what they wanted. He would have to hold out as long as he physically could. The only problem was that he really had created a superbug, and it was now weaponized. Sorenson had to keep that little secret to himself no matter what.

Sure, the discovery had been an accident, but then most scientific advances were. The problem was that it shouldn't have worked, but it had. Tristan still had only a vague idea of how he had managed to turn what was supposed to be a benign flu bug into an anti-viral superweapon.

His captives had beaten the hell out of him, and he was pretty sure that they had at least cracked a few of his ribs. Sorenson gasped in pain as he tried to take a deep breath. He didn't know for sure who his captives were, but he had his suspicions. He had seen the hulking leader before. Dante Schultz was a Neo-Nazi. That meant that the man wanted to target Israel with the bug. The problem was, it wouldn't just infect Jews. It would infect anyone who came into contact with it. And it had a 99% fatality rate.

~ ~ ~

If turned loose on an unsuspecting world, it could mean the death of most humans on the face of the Earth! Somehow, Tristan had to figure out a way to stop Schultz from releasing it. The question was how?

~ ~ ~

Gina had purchased sunglasses and a hat to try and change her appearance. While she waited to meet her supposed protector. She shook her head as she took a seat on a bench out in front of the Government Center. She would give it half an hour and then she would run. Head north for the border and try to make her way to the United States. Maybe, if she made it that far, she would finally be safe.

Storm arrived earlier than the pick-up time. He wanted to get eyes on the woman and make sure that she hadn't been followed. Within ten minutes, he knew she was clean. Storm started walking towards her to make his approach. Nick approached the bench and took a seat at the opposite end of the bench.

The girl gave him a nervous glance when he first sat down but made no move to speak. Instead, she sat there fidgeting with her hands. That wasn't good, because it would draw attention to her from passersby. "Would you happen to have the time, Miss?" Storm asked her. She jumped slightly, startled by the question from a stranger.

"Uh," Gina glanced at her watch. "Five o'clock," Gina told him.

"I'm here to help. I'm looking for Doctor Sorenson too," Nick told her.

"Prove it," Gina hissed. Her whole body was suddenly tense, already primed for flight if need be.

"You called a certain number that Tristan had given you if anything happened to him. I'm the one he sent to pick you up and protect you," Nick told her, keeping his voice low enough that none or the passerby's could hear him. Gina took a deep breath and let it out slowly.

"Let's get out of here," Gina whispered. Nick stood up and took her hand as she stood. They walked off together, looking for all the world like a married couple. Nick kept his eyes moving as they walked to his rental car. Nobody seemed to be showing any untoward interest in them. He opened the car door and ushered her inside before closing the door and walking around to the driver's side. Within seconds, they were driving away to what Nick hoped would be the relative safety of his hotel.

"So, who are you?" Gina asked after they were on the road.

"Noah Stark. You are?" he asked, having fed her his cover legend.

"Gina Torres. Tristan and I worked together at Microbe LLC."

"I heard. Your colleagues spoke highly of you. And your close relationship with Doctor Sorenson," Nick told her.

"I'll bet they did. They were pretty jealous that I never gave a one of them a tumble. Tristan was different. He saw me for who I was and not just as some brainless bimbo assigned to the lab for her looks," Gina replied.

"That tracks with what they told me back at the lab. It's gone by the way, burnt to the ground. Those people don't like loose ends," Nick sighed.

"No, they don't. I need to find Tristan. He had actually made a breakthrough that had made the virus that he was working with 100 times more dangerous than it had been before. It was weaponized. A super-fast airborne spreading virus that attacks the respiratory system like a reaper's scythe. He had also come up with an anti-virus that could be used as an antidote if delivered on time," Gina explained.

"Then we need to find him and do it double-damn quick," Nick told her.

Eight

The news that Sorenson had actually managed to weaponize what should have been a benign cold virus into a deadly bioweapon was not good news. It made finding Tristan Sorenson even more of a priority. He also needed to touch base with Riley and Dixon. After that, he'd call Jim King. He still didn't trust the CIA case officer any farther than he could throw the office buildings at Langley that housed the CIA.

"Gina, what else can you tell me?" Storm asked.

"There was a man that came around the lab every once in a while. Tristan was afraid of him, but tried hard not to show it. He said his name was Parker, but I got the feeling that he was actually working for someone else," Gina explained.

"What did this Parker look like?" Nick needed a description if he were to pass it along to Dixon. If anyone could identify the guy it was Dixon. Nick had more faith in him than he did the CIA.

"He was big, looked like a military type. Looked like he had trouble finding shirts that would fit him because of all the muscle. His head was shaved and his eyes were blue. He radiated an aura of quiet menace. I could understand why he scared Tristan. He scared me too," Gina replied.

"That is helpful. Okay, we are heading back to my hotel so I can pass that along to some friends of mine. They might be able to identify him," Nick explained.

"I hope so. Because right now, to put it delicately, I am officially scared shitless!" Gina told him.

"You are not the only one," Nick agreed with her. A weaponized bio-weapon that could wipe out most of the population on earth was out there in the wild in the hands of someone who was not afraid to use it. It was a very sobering thought. Nick drove them back to his hotel.

The clock was now ticking on this job, and Nick was starting to feel that he had gotten a late start on the race. Gina remained quiet on the drive, though Nick could tell she had a lot of questions. He hoped he might be able to answer a few of them, but he was doubtful of it.

"So, you work for the CIA?" Gina asked.

"Sometimes. I used to work for another agency but they got disbanded, so I took this job as a favor for an old friend. I guess you could say I freelance now," Nick shrugged.

"I bet," Gina nodded, not sure if she actually believed him or not. Still, he was the best shot she had at staying alive long enough to save Tristan. It took them about half an hour to reach his hotel. After locking the car, Nick led Gina into the hotel and up to his room.

Gina took note of the two queen-sized beds and was happy to know that they wouldn't have to share one. Gina took a seat on one of the beds as Nick walked to the safe and unlocked it to retrieve his laptop. He carried it to the desk and booted it up, and then he sent an encrypted signal to Key West to alert Larry Dixon that he had something. Within two minutes Dixon had fashioned an encrypted Zoom call.

Storm had Gina give Dixon the description of the suspected mercenary call Palmer. After telling them he would call back when he had something, Dixon signed off. Nick closed the laptop. He looked at Gina. "Are you hungry?"

"I could eat," Gina admitted.

"They have a pretty decent restaurant downstairs. Care to try it out?"

"Sounds good," Gina replied, offering him a quick smile.

~ ~ ~

Tristan Sorenson struggled against his bonds. He hoped that he wasn't just imagining that it felt like he was getting some slack in the rope around his wrists. The metal barracks-style building was hot and oppressive feeling more like an oven with the later in the day it got. One of his captors would come in and give him a few sips of water every hour or so to keep him from dehydrating. They refused to take him to the bathroom so he had been forced to sit in wet pants that were stained and smelled of his own urine.

The door opened and a man walked in. "Sorry for the inhospitable treatment, Dr. Sorenson. However, I don't believe that I can trust you not to try to escape. I'm well aware of the breakthrough that you have made in your research, but I want you to take it a step farther. My name is Dante Schultz and I am your host."

"Why did you kidnap me?" Sorenson asked.

"Because I need you to modify your virus again. I want you to modify it to attack certain racial types."

"Why would I do that?"

"Perhaps to spare your own life?" Schultz smiled with amusement.

"If I don't?"

"Then you will be patient zero in a world-wide pandemic that will end most life on earth," Schultz shrugged.

~ ~ ~

Sergeant Juan Lopez frowned at the desk clerk. "What do you mean that Nathan Simms is no longer here?"

"He left this morning and left his key in his room. He also left a note that he was returning to the United States and that he had completed his mission for the Center for Disease Control," the clerk shrugged in that way that Central and South American men had turned into a gesture of eloquence unparoled by any other humans on earth.

Lopez big off an angry curse. He would call the airport. There was still a chance that Simms had not yet left the country and could be pulled from his plane. Angry as much as with himself as he was at the clerk for the bad news, Lopez stalked out of the hotel.

Nathan Simms had lied to him. Lopez was sure of that. But how much of what the man said was a lie and how much was truth? Until he could talk to him face to face, he had no way to judge. He would head back to the office and call the CDC in Atlanta, Georgia. He would demand that they send Simms back if he had already managed to flee Costa Rica.

~ ~ ~

Gina and Storm had just finished their dinner when Nick's phone rang. Nick glanced at the screen. He recognized the number. It was Larry Dixon. Nick answered. "Talk to me," Nick said.

"Major Glenn Parker, former Delta Force operator turned mercenary. He has been operating in third world countries and selling himself to the highest bidder. He is a known associate of one Dante Schultz, head of a Neo-Nazi group of mercenaries that go by the name of Iron Cross. Iron Cross hires to anybody that can meet their price," Dixon explained.

"Anybody know who might have hired Iron Cross to kidnap the good doctor?" Nick asked.

"Not a one. Not yet, anyway. Give me a couple of hours and I might be able to figure it out," Dixon told him.

"I hope so," Nick replied before breaking the connection. He looked over at Gina. She was eyeing him expectantly. "After we get back to the room," he told her, hoping that would be enough. Gina nodded her agreement, putting her trust in him that he would keep his word.

~ ~ ~

Once they were back in his hotel room and he swept it for bugs, he finally told her to sit down and then he told her what Dixon had told him. "Nazi's?" Gina looked stunned.

"Yes. They are the kind of bad guys that crawl under rocks and then keep coming back years later. Iron Sky is that kind of group. They constantly turn up in brushfire wars and brokering weapons deals. Dante Schultz is the leader of Iron Sky. He's got a rap sheep longer than my leg," Nick explained.

"How exactly do you know this?"

"I work for the government, chasing down guys like Dante Schultz," Nick told her.

"Is Noah even your real name?"

"I could tell you, but then I'd have to kill you," Nick grinned, using the old special forces joke. It wasn't lost on Gina.

"Will you ever tell me your real name?"

"Maybe when this is all over."

"I think I might like that. But only after Tristan is safe," Gina told him.

"Of course. I wouldn't consider it any other way."

Dante Schultz looked up as Major Parker walked into the room. Schultz was angry about something. Parker figured it had to do with Tristan Sorenson and his bug. "Is there a problem?" Parker asked.

"Our guest is being less co-operative than I had thought he would be." Schultz replied with a scowl.

"Shall I speak to him?"

"There isn't time right now. We need to head north to Nicaragua. Our clients are waiting for delivery. I have no doubt that they will allow you to persuade him to co-operate in their demands."

"I certainly hope so," Parker smiled thinly.

"Get him ready to travel. No need to be gentle with him," Schultz said.

"My pleasure," Parker replied with a smile that actually looked dangerous.

"Have you ever heard of an organization called Iron Cross?" Nick asked Gina Torres.

"Not that I can recall," Gina shook her head. "Who are they?"

"They are a fringe Neo-Nazi group, very active in Central and South America. They claim to be children of the Fourth Reich, descendants of original Nazis that fled to South America at the end of World War Two, most of them steps ahead of firing squads for war crimes," Nick explained.

"Wow, what a wonderful group. But why would they be after Tristan?" Gina asked.

"They want to use his research as a weapon," Nick sighed.

"Oh my God!" Gina gasped, raising her hand to cover her mouth.

"That's why we need to find him and get him away from Iron Cross as soon as possible."

"You think you can do that?"

"I can tell you that I will do my best to do exactly that. But we have to find him first."

~ ~ ~

Key West, Florida USA.

Jack Riley stormed into the former Caribe Operations Center. Larry Dixon was sitting in his usual seat in front of a large bank of computer monitors. "What have you got, Larry?" Riley asked.

"Nick has stumbled into an Iron Cross operation. I know you have your own history with them," Dixon replied.

"That I did. Now, however, Nick is the one involved in having to deal with them. We need to back him up, officially or not," Riley said.

"I figured that already, Jack. Jay Barr is already in the area, and as is Meredith 'Mac" Mackenzie. Mac might be the better choice to help him in this particular instance than Jay."

"Mac is already in place and she has worked with Nick before. But putting those two together is like pouring gasoline on an open flame," Jack shook his head.

"True, but Jay only pilots. There is a chance that MacKenzie's expertise on the water might be more practical. Plus, checked, she's also jump-trained. She may be freelancing for the CIA, but she's kept her certifications up," Dixon countered.

"I dunno, Larry," Riley said, "This could cause more problems for Nick. He's already in Dutch with Jim King. Mac could blow the whole operation up. You know how she feels about Nazis."

"Yeah, she hates them like any normal person would. Much as I hate to say it, I actually trust her more than I do Jim King."

"Okay, I'll reach out to her to see if she is available, but no promises," Riley sighed.

"I never asked for any, Jack. I just offered a proposal," Dixon replied.

"Right," Jack Riley rolled his eyes as he turned and headed back to what had been his old office. Meredith Mackenzie was something of a wild card in any deck that contained her. She had been a great field operative, until one day she decided to walk away from it all and bought a boat and started working as a Marine Biologist, something she still had a degree in.

Mac had then began freelancing for a few intelligence agencies in the United States. Mac and her crew on *The Sea Chaser* had carried out contract work for not only the CIA, but the DEA, DOD, and NSA as well. Riley pulled her number up on his encrypted cell phone and hit the call button.

A voice answered two rings later. "Jack Riley to what do I owe the pleasure?" Meredith Mackenzie asked with just a hint of amusement in her voice. She knew that Riley was not a fan of hers, but she also knew that he valued her abilities in the field. She had heard that Caribe had been disbanded, so what did he want with her?

Nine

"Are you currently on a mission?" Jack's voice filled her ear.

"Why would you want to know?" Mac asked, her curiosity getting the better of her.

"Because Nick needs some back-up in Costa Rica. Iron Cross is involved," Riley replied.

"I thought Caribe was shut down. What the hell is Nick doing in Costa Rica?"

"Jim King hired him to find a virologist that disappeared from a lab down there. The guy was working on weaponizing a new virus. Then the scientist was kidnapped and all of his research was taken as well. King had sent a couple of other people down, but they ended up dead and King came looking for Nick. Nick was getting bored and took the job," Riley explained.

"I'm near Cozumel. Just dropped off a charter there. Do you need *The Sea Chaser* as well?" Mac asked.

"Just you for the moment, but it might not be a bad idea to have your boat in the area," Riley replied.

"If Jay is in the area, have him come and pick me up. I'll have Fiona and Ezra take *The Sea Chaser* in closer to Nicaragua if we need a quick extraction. Does Nick know that I'm going to be joining him?" Mac asked.

"Not yet, no. But I'm pretty sure he's going to need you," Riley sighed.

"Why?'

"Because he doesn't trust Jim King and neither do I."

"Good for your both," Mac replied before hanging up. She would need to put together a gear bag before Barr arrived to pick her up. The pilot was a salty old fart, but she liked him just the same.

She understood the distrust of Jim King. She didn't trust him either. She had only operated with him one time and it had turned into a full-blown clusterfuck and she had barely made it out with her life. So, if Jim King were involved, then Nick would need all of the help that he could get.

~ ~ ~

Nick and Gina had reached the hotel and gone to his room. Nick had checked the tell-tales that he had put in place to alert him if anyone had entered his room. They were all still in place. Gina took a seat on one of the beds as Nick unlocked the room safe and pulled out his laptop.

"What now?" Gina asked as she watched him open the laptop and boot it up.

"Now I contact my handler and see if they can help us with figuring this out," Storm told her.

"Do you think that will help?" Gina asked.

"It might. We won't know until we try."

~ ~ ~

Jack Riley answered on the first ring. "Nick where are you?"

"At a new hotel on the northern end of San Jose. I have Gina Torres here with me. She was Sorenson's research assistant," Storm replied.

"Any sign of Iron Cross?"

"Not that I can prove. I'm pretty sure that they are the ones that took Sorenson. However, I don't have any real proof other than video that I copied from the lab before it went up in flames. I already sent that to Dixon."

"I've got you some back-up heading your way, just in case. Dante Schultz and his boys are a dangerous bunch."

"You think I don't know that? I've dealt with neo-Nazi groups before. They hate to play nice. Who are you sending?" Storm asked, suddenly wary.

"Mac is on her way to you. Jay is bringing her to you."

"Are you out of your ever-loving mind?" Storm snapped.

"There is a chance that King is a double agent, Nick. You need somebody you can trust to watch your back. Mac is the only person close," Riley replied.

"Well shit!" Storm exploded

"Think about it Nick. Would you really want to take on Iron Cross with little to no back-up? You already told me you don't trust King after he bugged your old room twice," Riley said. Nick clenched his fist. He hated when Riley was right.

"Fine, but she is back-up only. I don't need her trying to take over this operation."

"She understands that."

"I hope so," Nick said before ending the call.

"So, who is this Mac you were talking about?" Gina asked, her curiosity getting the better of her. All of this spy versus spy stuff was giving her a headache.

"Mac is an ex-partner as well as an ex-girlfriend. We don't always get along."

"Given your charm? How could that be?" Gina rolled her eyes.

"Hard to believe I know," Nick told her, grinning as he did.

~ ~ ~

Jim King frowned. Storm had dropped off the grid, which meant that he had probably gone rogue. That couldn't be allowed to happen. No, Jim needed Storm on a short leash until Iron Cross was safely out of the country with Sorenson and his materials.

Dante Schultz was paying him a great deal to make that happen. So, now he had to figure out what to do about the former Caribe agent. This whole plan had come about back at Foggy Bottom at the end of Caribe's last mission. King's boss had been one of the people who wanted the upstart task force disbanded. This job was supposed to drive the final nail into Caribe's coffin.

Now it was all going south on him. Given Nick Storm's reputation from his CIA days, King knew that he should have expected it. However, there might a way to fix it all. King grinned as he pulled out his cell phone and dialed the San Juan Police Department. When they picked up, he asked for Sergeant Lopez. Storm had mentioned that the cop had been very suspicious of him. Lopez might just well be the solution to his problem.

~ ~ ~

Sergeant Lopez had driven to San Jose, searching for the suddenly missing CDC scientist going by the name of Nathan Simms. An anonymous tip had let him know that the man was some sort of spy. That begged the question of who he was working for and what was his interest in the missing scientist really about?

Lopez didn't like being made a fool of, and Nathan Simms had done exactly that. He didn't like spies working in his country in general, but to have been made a fool by one was the highest of insults. The fact that Simms had uncovered something about Sorenson's disappearance and hadn't shared it was worse.

Lopez was headed for the hotel that Simms had stayed at in to question the staff to see if they had noticed anything suspicious about his behavior or any visitors that might have looked Simms up.

~ ~ ~

Washington, D.C. United States.
Senator Blake Dern frowned at the telephone on his desk. The call that he had just received was most disturbing. Sorenson was not co-operating, at least not according to Schultz. Senator Dern had hired Iron Cross to kidnap the scientist. Dern's grandparents had escaped Nazi Germany before the war had ended, using the Odessa pipeline to reach Argentina. They had then migrated to the United States and still raised him to believe the Nazi doctrine. At least in private. They had made sure that he had prospered in his political endeavors.

Now he was a Senator and on the United States Intelligence Oversite Committee. He had helped fund Sorenson's research into weaponizing the virus. Now, Sorenson was refusing to mutate it to attack a specific DNA type. Dern had already contacted some friends in Venezuela that had the expertise to do what Sorenson refused. As far as Dern was concerned, Tristan Sorenson was no longer needed.

~ ~ ~

Costa Rica.

Jim King had sicced Lopez on Storm's trail. Now all he could do was wait and pray that the cop caught Storm before he fucked things up further. So far, King had managed to hide his actions from Langley, but he realized that he wouldn't be able to do that much longer. Soon, King knew, he would have to cut his losses and drop out of sight permanently. Because if his associating with Iron Cross came out, King was as good as dead. He was guilty of treason already, and that carried the death penalty. Being exposed as a double agent would put the crosshairs firmly on his back.

King was already planning his escape. He had three passports that the Agency knew nothing about. He had made sure to use a reliable source unknown to his CIA bosses to create the new identities for him. All were fully back-stopped and were easily adapted to. He had siphoned off cash from his operational funds and sent it to his off-shore secret accounts.

The only thing keeping him from cutting and running was not knowing where Storm was hiding and how much the man had figured out. Not knowing was driving him nuts. Iron Cross mercenaries were scouring San Jose for any sign of Storm, but so far, they were coming up empty. That was something that King couldn't afford, leaving a loose end like Nick Storm behind him.

~ ~ ~

Nick had packed them up and they were heading north in a stolen car that he had swapped the license plates with another vehicle before they had left San Jose behind them. They would be meeting Mac in Barranca. Jay Barr was flying her in there.

Gina had insisted that they fill the car with gas and they had stopped at a store to purchase food for the trip. Now, Nick was eating a sandwich that she had made Storm after they hit the road heading north and west. The plan was to slip into Nicaragua near La Paz. Hopefully Riley and Dixon would have a location on where Iron Cross had taken Sorenson.

There was a possibility that Mac might be able give them an update when she joined them, but Nick wasn't going to count on it. No, plan for worst and be happy if it didn't go south. That was what he had to hold onto. He chuckled to himself as he remembered a saying that a former Navy SEAL had told him. The hardest day was yesterday.

He glanced at Gina. She seemed to be taking this all a lot better than he would have thought. He made a mental note to have Dixon do a deep dive into her background. If she was hiding something, he needed to know sooner than later.

~ ~ ~

Tristan Sorenson spat blood onto the floorboards in the back of the truck that he was tied up in. Major Parker had seemed to take a certain delight in inflicting pain on him, but did so in ways that would not impede his survival. Sorenson was pretty sure that the man was a sociopath based on his behavior so far. Schultz was worse though, he was a full-blown psychopath, but then most Nazis were.

Every bump in the road sent shockwaves of pain through his body. Still, the pain helped him realize that he was still alive, and if he was alive, he still had a chance to escape. Still, at the moment it wasn't looking too good. There were four armed Nazis in the back of the Duce and a half with him underneath the canvas covering.

~ ~ ~

Mac had stayed quiet during most of the flight, knowing that Barr was not exactly a fan of small talk. Instead, she watched the countryside passing by beneath them. There was a lot of rain forest down there. She was concerned for Nick. They had once been lovers, but that had ended long ago. Still, she had never gotten over the feelings that she still had for him. "We are getting close to Barranca," Barr informed her through the headset.

"Good to know," Mac answered.

"Are you sure you want to do this?" the pilot asked, showing some uncustomary concern.

"I am. I owe Nick a lot. This will help clear the tab," Mac replied. The helicopter dropped down low over the roof of a tall building. Barr hovered about a yard over the flat rooftop. Mac tossed out her backpack and then dropped down beside it in a crouch. She gave Barr a wave and the helicopter lifted off and headed back towards the Atlantic side of the country.

Mac scooped up her pack after the helicopter had headed away from her and slipped it on her back. She was dressed like a tourist, khaki cargo pants, hiking boots, and a tank top over a sports bra. Her suppressed pistol was inside a hidden pocket in the O.D. green backpack she now wore. She had a fast-assisted opening knife with a six-inch blade in one pocket, a tactical pen in the other. There was also an ASP expandable baton in one of the cargo pockets of her pants.

It would be easy enough to defend herself if the need should arise. She also had an encrypted iPhone that had come pre-loaded with Storm's number. She would wait to call until she had secured a place for them to stay for the night. After that, all that Mac could do was wait.

~ ~ ~

Gina had fallen asleep, lured by the hum of the tires on the highway. Nick was glad that she had fallen asleep. He was still not sure if he trusted her or not. It was well possible that Mac might have some insight into this woman who had been Tristan Sorenson's research assistant.

Ten

Meredith McKenzie had made her way to the rendezvous point and was sitting in an outdoor café drinking water from a bottle when she spotted Storm. He was dressed all touristy in khaki Cargo pants and wearing an Aloha shirt over an undershirt that had somehow picked up the title of wife-beater. She shook her head. Seeing him still made her heart beat a little faster. His dark hair was a little longer than she had remembered, but she still recognized his walk despite the baseball cap and dark sunglasses that covered his face.

Nick walked up and took a seat where he could at least partially have a wall at his back. He figured Mac could keep an eye out behind him as he would do with her. "So, bring me up to date," Mac suggested.

"Sorenson was kidnapped, most likely by Iron Cross mercenaries. They came after me when I was searching his lab and burnt the whole place to the ground. I've got a cop from Limon on my backtrail. I also have Sorenson's lab assistant camped out in the hotel. I think she knows more than she has told me, so I want to turn her over to you for questioning. I suspect she will tell you more than she will me," Storm explained.

"You're probably right. Women are far more likely to confide in another woman, even a stranger, than a man who she barely knows," Mac replied.

"I hope you are right," Storm sighed. "I'll give you two some alone time up in the room."

"And just what will you be doing while we have our girl-talk?"

"Keeping an eye out for trouble," Nick replied.

~ ~ ~

Washington, D.C.

Jack Riley had flown up from Key West to D.C. He had a meeting scheduled with the President. He was hoping that the Man would listen to what he had to say. Dixon had discovered a link between a highly-placed Senator and the terrorist group Iron Cross. All Riley had to do was convince the President that the Senator was a traitor. That was not going to be easy, even with the evidence that Dixon had uncovered and copied.

Riley was still on the government payroll, despite Caribe being at least temporarily disbanded. Though now he carried the title of advisor to the President. Riley had a plan to keep Caribe alive, but it would all hinge on the success or failure of Nick Storm's current mission in Costa Rica.

Foggy bottom was foggier than usual these days. Too much had happened over the past couple of years. The Covid pandemic hadn't helped, nor had the toxic division of the two major political parties. Riley was concerned about a possible civil war if some moderation or compromise couldn't be reached.

Riley shook his head. He needed to concentrate on his reason for being at the White House. Dixon would inform him if there was any news from Storm. Riley stepped out of the limousine that had carried him from the airport to the White House. He greeted the two Secret Service agents that met him and escorted him inside.

~ ~ ~

Costa Rica.

Nick was feeling restless. They should have already been on the road to La Paz. It would help to know what Gina Torres knew, but in his opinion, it was taking too long. To hell with it! Nick turned the corner heading back to the hotel when he spotted a familiar face on the street out front. Sergeant Lopez, the pain in the ass cop from back down in Limon. How the hell had he managed to track him. Then it hit him.

Jim King had betrayed him and sold him out. He had suspected that it was coming, he just hadn't thought it would happen this quick. He had to catch Lopez and put him out of commission long enough for them to get out of the country. Shit! This could not have happened at a worse time. Jim King was not going to like what happened to him once Storm caught up to him.

Storm pulled the bill of his cap and began to move in behind Lopez as he entered the building. The lobby was actually empty except for the two of them. Good. That would make things easier. They walked towards the elevator and Nick punched the button for the floor above his, then stepped back so Lopez could choose his floor. He pressed the button for the floor that Nick had registered his legend on. The doors opened and Lopez stepped out. Nick was right behind him. Luckily, there was nobody in the hall.

Storm drew out his tactical pen and struck Lopez at the base of his skull, dropping the cop like a pole-axed steer. Nick caught him before he hit the floor and dragged him to the room. Once they had him inside, Mac helped Nick tie the cop up and gagged him with a towel. "What are you going to do with him?" Gina asked, her eyes growing wide.

"Leave him tied up in here. He's a cop just doing his job. Unfortunately, his job interferes with mine, thus his current situation," Nick replied.

"You are saying we need to get the hell out of Dodge, aren't you?" Mac asked.

"You could say that, and you'd be right. We need to get out of Costa Rica. The last word I had is that Iron Cross is moving him across the border tonight. La Paz is the closest border crossing."

"So, what are y'all waiting for?" Mac grinned at him.

~ ~ ~

Ten minutes later, they were on the road. Nick figured that they had maybe an hour before a maid found Lopez tied up and set him free. They needed to be much closer to La Paz before that happened.

Nick frowned as he drove. They had covered several miles and were getting close to the border with Nicaragua. He was getting a bad feeling the closer that they were getting to the border. Mac picked up on his anxiety. She had worked with him in the past and could read him like a damned book. He hated that.

"What's up, Nick?" Mac asked.

"I have a bad feeling about crossing the border in the open. I have a feeling that the enemy is going to be watching for us.," Storm told her.

"I have a plan," Mac grinned at him.

"Of course, you do," Nick rolled his eyes. Mac was an excellent strategist. Nick couldn't deny that. He was fairly certain that he knew what she was going to suggest.

~ ~ ~

Washington, D.C.

"Are you serious about this Jack? Blake Dern may be an asshole, but a Nazi? The President shook his head, uncertain if he believed it or not.

"Sir, I wouldn't be here if I wasn't sure of what I was bringing you. Doctor Sorenson was working on weaponizing a fairly harmless virus for the CDC. Then he was kidnapped by the Neo-Nazi terrorist group calling themselves Iron Cross, and all of his research was taken as well."

"Plus, my computer guy did a deep dive on Blake Dern's past. Dern was actually born in Argentina, in a town that was set up by Nazi who had fled to Argentina from Germany at the end of World War Two," Riley explained. The Commander in Chief nodded his head.

"Look into Dern, then. Find me uncontrivable proof to take Dern down. And pray that your man in Central America stops Iron Cross from releasing that virus! Covid -19 was bad enough. The Country cannot afford another pandemic this soon after the last one.

"There is one other thing. Blake Dern has a son, also born in Argentina. His son, we believe is the head of Iron Phoenix," Jack added.

"Find proof, Jack," The President told him.

~ ~ ~

Costa Rica.

Nick stopped the car in a small coastal town a few miles below the border with Nicaragua. La Paz wasn't far away, but Mac had come up with a plan to get them into Nicaragua that didn't include a border crossing station. She had put it in motion before she had left *The Sea Chaser.*

Nick had to give it to Mac, she was good, always thinking two or three steps ahead. He remembered that she had won a college chess championship. He smiled at the memory. They had been working together on a job in Europe, stalking a Russian FSB assassin when Mac had told him about winning the chess tournament. After that, Nick had let Mac plan the operation and they had successfully taken the Russian out. Since then, he always deferred to her when it came to planning their missions.

~ ~ ~

"When is your crew due in?" Storm asked as he parked the car in front of a small restaurant and marina. Mac glanced her watch before answering.

"About twenty-minutes or so," Mac replied.

"How about we take time to go to the bathroom and get a bite to eat? That was a really bumpy ride coming up here from San Jose," Gina reminded them.

"That's a good idea," Mac agreed.

"I'll order the food. How do y'all feel about fish tacos?" Nick asked.

"Those will work," both women agreed before heading to find a restroom. Nick shook his head. Still, finding a restroom first might not be a bad idea. He spotted assign that identified the men's room in English and several other languages. Storm sighed and stepped through the doorway.

It wasn't but a moment until the distant sound of helicopter rotors sounded from the southeast. The chopper was an old Vietnam era Huey troopship. It dropped down a block from the marina and a dozen men in military style gear jumped out. The chopper lifted back off as the soldiers unlimbered their weapons and started for the marina after separating into a skirmish line. Each of them wore armbands on their left arm emblazoned with an eagle over a swastika. Mac had just stepped outside and spotted the armed group heading towards the restaurant and the marina. "Crap," she said, easing back inside, backing into Gina Torres.

"What's wrong?"

"We have a major problem."

"What?"

"Iron Phoenix has found us," Mac sighed.

"What can we do?"

"Stay hid and stay quiet while I figure that out," Mac replied.

~ ~ ~

Nick had recognized the sound of an approaching helicopter as he stepped inside. Since he was already there, he quickly took care of business. Then he drew his Ruger EC9mm and eased the door open enough for him to see what was coming. Storm immediately spotted the red armbands and knew who the armed men belonged to. Getting out of the cinder-block restroom was now a priority. He could only hope that Mac and Gina were safe.

Storm eased the door open and slipped behind the building. The sun was sinking over the Pacific Ocean and darkness was falling. Storm took stock of what he had. Seven rounds in his gun and 14 more in the two spare magazines in his cargo pocket. Not much to take on a squad of trained commandos. He also had his fast-opening combat pocket knife, if he could get close enough to use it. Nick pulled out his suppressor and screw it onto the threaded barrel of his pistol. It might help him keep the element of surprise for a few more minutes.

~ ~ ~

Wolfgang Schroder was leader of Iron Phoenix kill team. The black BDU uniforms helped his men blend into the shadows of the small sea-side town. A few weak streetlights were starting to flicker on but they didn't provide much in the way of actual illumination.

Something to be thankful for. Schroder spotted the car that the American agent was said to be driving. It was parked outside a small restaurant in front of boat docks. Weak bulbs barely illuminated the wooden docks and the boats tied up there.

This should be an easy mission, like shooting fish in a barrel. Then he heard the quiet chunk-chunk of a pistol slide racking. Something struck his left shoulder and spun him around. Schroder triggered his throat mike. "Taking fire, engage!" he commanded. Then all hell broke loose.

~ ~ ~

Mac and Gina had slipped outside and scurried behind another building as the soldiers began to encircle the restaurant. Mac had her pistol in hand as she worked her way around the building next to the restaurant. The bad guys were getting in position, then suddenly one of them fell spinning to the ground. The man gave an order and the rest of his team opened fire on the restaurant. Shattering glass and screams filled the night air, mostly coming from inside the building. Mac fired two shots, dropping the man closest to her. She ran in a crouch to his body and yanked his H&K MP5 loose from his body. She snatched a couple of spare magazines for the submachine gun and then darted back for cover. She watched as two men on the other side of the building went down.

Mac raised the MP5 and flipped the fire selector for 3-round burst and promptly took down three more men. More fire erupted and soon the guns fell silent. Mac eased out from cover and approached the fallen bodies. She stopped next to the first man that had fallen and kicked his weapons away. He glared up at her with hate-filled eyes.

"You will pay for this," he snarled. Mac kicked him in the side of the head and sent him to la-la-land. Nick approached her.

"We will take this one with us since he seemed to be in charge," Storm told her.

"Good idea. Maybe he can tell us something about Sorenson and his location," Mac agreed. Just then, her phone buzzed. "Go," Mac said.

"When you throw a party, you don't kid around, do you Boss?" Fiona Scott asked.

"Are you here?" Mac asked.

"Pulling up to the dock as we speak," Fiona replied.

"Be ready to go as soon as we get aboard. I'm pretty sure that we have worn out our welcome around here."

"Aye-aye, Boss. *Sea Chaser* out," Fiona replied.

"You grab Gina and I'll handle Hans here," Storm told her after he flex-cuffed Schroder's hands behind his back, then he helped him up and shoved him towards the docks.

Eleven

Sean Jacobs and Ezra James helped them get their prisoner and Gina Torres aboard *The Sea Chaser* while Fiona backed the boat away from the dock. Fiona spun the wheel and headed back out to sea as she engaged the throttles. The boat headed back out into the Pacific Ocean.

"Thanks for the quick pick-up," Mac told Fiona as she walked onto the bridge.

"Just doing my job, Captain," Fiona replied, turning the controls over to her boss.

"Right."

"So, who are our guests?"

"Are you sure you want to know?"

"I hate it went you answer my questions with a question."

"Why do you think I do it?" Mac grinned. "Let's just say that Jack Riley needed me to help Nick out of a tight spot."

"You mean hot Nick?"

"I mean Nick Storm," Mac rolled her eyes.

"That's who I meant," Fiona grinned back. Then the ship's engineer left the wheelhouse. Mac shook her head. She knew that Fiona had developed a crush on the Caribe agent the last time they had worked together. She hoped that it wouldn't be a problem on this current job. She pulled up the navigation computer and plotted a course that would have them off the coast of La Paz in under two hours.

"Nick, it's been a while," Sean Jacobs said as the dropped the Iron Cross mercenary into a chair.

"That it has. Still enjoying being a CIA liaison with Adventure Incorporated?" Nick asked.

"For the most part. Captain Mackenzie can be a little hard to handle."

Nick snorted.   "I warned you about that."

"Yes, you did. What's the story on this guy?"

"Neo-Nazi, works for Iron Cross. His group kidnapped a virologist and his research from Limon and took his research. The virus was weaponized with a 98% mortality rate. From what we can tell, they are taking him to a hidden base on Nicaragua to further mutate it. Jim King sent me on this mission and then hung me out to dry," Nick explained.

"Jim King? You are lucky to be alive. He has a reputation for putting his agents into harm's way," Sean told him.

"That's why I wasn't really surprised. Which was why I had my old boss back me up," Nick said.

"Smart move," Jacobs nodded.

"I thought so. I knew King's reputation and new some of the agents he had left hung out to dry. I'm fairly sure that King has ties to Iron Cross himself."

"Can you use another hand on this?" Sean asked.

"Are you offering?"

"Yeah, I am. I've got a bone to pick with Jim King and it sounds like this would be the perfect opportunity to do something about it."

"It sounds good to me," Nick told him. "Now, I gotta contact my old boss and see if they can give us a location of where Iron Cross might be holding Sorenson." Nick carried his laptop and headed for the wheelhouse.

Mac was at the wheel when he plopped his laptop down on the chart table and opened it up. The laptop was a military-grade ruggedized type with an antenna the gave it satellite capability. Nick booted it up and opened up an encrypted channel to Dixon back on Key West.

"What have you got, Nick?" Larry Dixon's gruff voice filled the bridge.

"We've got one of the terrorists to interrogate, but we need to know where Iron Phoenix is headed with Dr. Sorenson sooner rather than later," Nick explained.

"Jack is up in D.C. right now. But he left instructions for you," Dixon told them.

"What are the instructions?" Nick asked.

"Do whatever it takes to stop those guys."

"Thanks, Dixon," Nick replied ending the call. He looked at Jacobs. "Looks like we need to go talk to our guest."

Wolfgang Schroder struggled against his bonds. He needed to get free. He had failed in his mission to kill the American agent. He deserved to die. Perhaps, he could get his captors to kill him if he played things right. Dante Schultz would have him executed on sight for failing to kill the American agent. No, he needed to find a way to find a way to get his captors to kill him before Iron Cross found him.

~ ~ ~

Nick noted that Schroder was struggling against his bonds when he entered the room. "You won't get loose," Nick told him.

"I have to try. Can't make things too easy for you," Schroder snarled at him.

"Where is Tristan Sorenson?"

"No place where you will find him. He might ever be dead already."

"For your sake, you better hope not."

"Why would it matter to me?"

"Because the local lady with me, that's Sorenson's girlfriend. She wants me to give her a knife and turn her loose on you. Said something about being descended from an Incan priestess. They did human sacrifices. Did you know that?" Nick asked softly.

"What do you mean, human sacrifices?" Schroder was starting to sweat.

"Part of their religious ceremonies. They would take a person and tie them to an altar, and then cut their still beating heart out of their chest and then eat it raw while the sacrifice was still alive and could see them," Nick shrugged.

"You would let her do that?" Schroder's eyes were wide.

"You took her man. I'm not sure that I could stop her if I tried. Honestly, she scares me."

At that moment, Gina entered the room and glared at the Neo-Nazi. "Has he talked yet?" she asked.

"Not yet," Nick replied, not taking his eyes off the man. Gina moved closer.

"Let me have him. I have my sacrificial dagger with me. Pure obsidian that had a blade hammered to razor sharpness," Gina almost whispered. It cuts as well as the finest steel!" Gina and Nick had planned all of it, but Schroder didn't know that.

"Give me another ten minutes. If he hasn't talked by then, you can have him," Nick told her.

"Are you fucking crazy?" Schroder almost screamed. The man was terrified. It took all Nick had to suppress a grin.

"No. But if you are ready to talk, I'm ready to listen," Nick told him.

"Fine," Schroder rolled his eyes. "Just keep her the hell away from me!"

~ ~ ~

"Head for La Paz," Nick told Mac as he walked into the bridge.

"He talked then?" Mac asked.

"He sang like the proverbial canary. Gina is quite the actress," Nick chuckled.

"I bet. Is there a specific place in La Paz we are looking for?"

"Yes, but unfortunately it is not on the waterfront. We'll have to go inland to get to it try to pull Sorenson out."

"Okay. So, what all do you need?"

"You and Sean. Ezra and Fiona can keep an eye on Gina and our guest," Nick replied.

"It sounds like you have a plan, then?"

"Yes. Though I'm not exactly sure that you are going to like it."

"Why should this time be any different?" Mac sighed.

Schroder had given them pretty good directions to the Iron Phoenix compound in the jungle north of La Paz. Gina had literally scared the crap out of the Neo-Nazi when she pulled out an actual obsidian dagger. It was one that she had bought in a gift shop, but Schroder had no way of knowing that. Mac had been impressed by the ingenuity of the way Nick and Gina had played the Neo-Nazi.

She had always known that Nick Storm had a devious mind. She had just never realized how devious. Of course, she didn't know Gina very well, but she did like the woman. Mac pulled her baseball cap down low over her eyes as she piloted the Zodiac Rigid Inflatable Boat towards shore. Nick and Sean were behind her and checking their weapons for the retrieval of Tristan Sorenson from the Iron Cross compound.

Mac shook her head. She had never pictured herself raiding a Neo-Nazi compound in the jungles of Nicaragua. This was something that belonged in some spy novel or a movie. Leave it to Nick and Jack Riley to pull her into something like this.

"Penny for your thoughts," Nick said from beside her.

"Keep the change," Mac replied with a grin.

"Wow. You wound me, Mac."

"No, but if you keep it up I might."

It was night, the main light coming from a half-moon above and the stars. Any other time, it would seem romantic. But not this time. This time, the three of them were out to stop a mad-man from killing off most of the population on the planet. Mac guided the RIB onto a sandy beach bordered by thick jungle.

Nick and Sean jumped off and towed the Zodiac up onto the beach as Mac shut down the engine and raised it so the prop wouldn't drag through the sand. Mac jumped out and helped them drag the boat up into the trees where they quickly camouflaged it and gathered their weapons and packs.

Nick led their way into the jungle. Based on what Schroder had told them, the base was at least a mile inland. Nick figured they should be able to reach the perimeter before daylight. He would have preferred to have more time to study the compound and get familiar with the routine. However, that just wasn't in the cards. The three of them needed to locate and extract Tristan Sorenson from the hands of Dante Schultz and Iron Cross.

"According to Gina, Sorenson had already found a way to weaponize the virus. It has an almost 100% mortality rate when anybody gets exposed to it. Iron Cross took his lab samples and all of his research materials. They would have no problem releasing it on the world. We can't let that happen," Nick explained as they stopped for a short break.

The Caribe operative glanced at his watch. They had about an hour before sunrise. They would have to be in place before then. If they had any hope of getting Sorenson and destroying the virus before the Neo-Nazi terrorist either used it or sold it to the highest bidder, they had to do it today!

A night-time infiltration would be better, but they didn't have time for that. No, they would have to do the extraction by daylight and hope for the best. It really wasn't much of a plan, but it was the best that they had at the moment, so they would just have to go with the flow and see what happened.

"Well, we're packing enough gear for an army, so I for one, hope that we don't need it all," Sean sighed.

"Buckle up, Buttercup. Let's get there and see what we can see," Mac grinned. Nick shook his head. Mac was an adrenaline junkie. Not so different from Nick himself.

~ ~ ~

Tristan groaned. His entire face was swollen so badly that he could barely open his eyes. Parker had beaten him within an inch of his life. Based on the pain he was feeling, he wasn't sure that he wouldn't die anyway. The last time that Parker had punched him, Tristan had felt something break inside him. He was pretty sure that he might be dying. His payment for tampering with nature and turning something benign into a deadly weapon. Schultz wanted him to refine it further, to make attack one specific race. Sorenson had refused. He had suffered for it, but he knew it was the right thing to do.

~ ~ ~

Dante Schultz paced back and forth in his office. The interrogation of their guest had not been as fruitful as he had hoped. So, it was time for plan B. There was a knock on his door. "Come," Schultz said.

The door opened and another bald man entered. His back was straight and his shoulders were squared. A dueling scar was cut down the left side of his face. He wore a monocle over his left eye. "Is the prisoner cooperating?" the man asked.

Dante Schultz studied the man for a long moment. This was the first time that he had met Dieter Bern in the flesh. Most of their communication had been via Zoom or encrypted text messages. Bern was the de-facto head of Iron Cross. Schultz squared his shoulders and faced his boss. "He is not cooperating at all, despite Major Parker's best efforts."

"He no longer matters. I am versed in the science of his research. I will do what he refuses to do," Bern replied.

"So, what do we do with Sorenson?" Schultz asked, certain that he already knew the answer.

"Kill him," Bern replied. "Now, take me to the lab so I can further mutate the virus to target the Jews."

Twelve

Humping 80 pounds of gear over rough ground and through a tropical rain forest was not exactly Nick's idea of fun. But the mission would require every ounce of equipment that they were hauling. The tropical heat and humidity were brutal, and they stopped often to take salt tabs and drink water. Nick was carrying an H&K MP-5 9mm submachine gun. Mac and Sean both carried M-4s, the latest version of the venerable m-16 chambered in 5.56.mm or .223 round. Between the three of them, they had enough explosives to take down an army base.

Of course, that was exactly what they planned to do. However, this was an unofficial base that was also a terrorist training center. Destroying the Iron Cross compound would give him a certain amount of satisfaction. Storm hated Nazis and all they stood for.

The sky was pink with the rising sun when they reached a small hill that over-looked the compound. Nick sent Mac to the north end of the camp and Sean to the south end. They both knew the plan and would get things set up. Once that was done, they would let him know and then he would breach the perimeter and yank Tristan Sorenson out of there and they would make a run for the coast and *The Sea Chaser.*

The three had separated with Sean and Mac heading for opposite ends of the camp. Mac would be concentrating on the motor pool and fuel storage. Sean would take the weapon's storage area. Nick would watch the camp and see exactly where Sorenson was being held.

Storm slithered his way close to the chain-link fence that surrounded the compound. He checked for wires and resisters that would be visible if it was electrified. None to be found. That was a good thing. Nick crawled using knees, and elbows to reach the perimeter of the fence. He pulled out a multitool and clipped enough wires that he could slip through when the diversions started.

~ ~ ~

It took a few minutes, but Sean found the weapons and ammo depot. He set three claymore mines in a semi-circle that when they exploded, would set off all of the munitions stored in the tent. There were also a few vehicles nearby that would also blow and add to the confusion and hopefully give Storm time to find and rescue Sorenson.

Sean didn't care for Jim King. He had worked with the guy and had gotten screwed over to the point that he had barely escaped with his life. The mission had been in Africa, back in the early 2000's Sean Jacob's team were set to terminate a rebel leader that was attempting a coup. King was supposed to be running the operation. On that particular day, King had been absent from the field, which was a little unusual.

Jacob's team was to make the touch and then ex-filtrate to a nearby airfield where a helicopter was supposed to pick them up and fly them out of the country. The rebel leader had never showed, but instead a lot of troops had. Sean ordered his team to fall back and meet at the airfield. Except, the army was waiting at the airfield. Jacob's team was captured and killed, except for Jacob and his spotter Abe Connors. They had managed to fight their way to the coast and catch a ride on a tramp steamer. Yes, Sean Jacobs had good reason to want to kill Jim King if the opportunity arose. He really hoped it would.

~ ~ ~

The motor pool wasn't very busy, something that worked to Meredith McKenzie's advantage. The near total lack of personnel there allowed her to wriggle under the fence and place her explosives where they would do the best job, and cause the most destruction. Once she had them all in place and armed, she slipped back out and into the jungle. She found a spot nearby that would give her the best field of fire once things started to happen.

Mac settled into wait for Nick's signal. Once she had that, all hell would rain down on the compound and she would start taking out any of the troops that emerged from the various tents or shacks. She knew that Sean would be doing the same at the other end of the camp while Nick found Sorenson and got him out. Then, the four of them would bug out for the coast and the Zodiac and then out to *The Sea Chaser.*

~ ~ ~

Dieter Bern sat on a chair in the make-shift lab and studied the research notes on the virus. The refinement that he wanted could be done quite easily. Sorenson really was brilliant. The man had taken a run of the mill cold virus and turned it into a deadly super-weapon. With very little tampering, he could make it target racial DNA. Bern smiled. It was a terrible thing to see. Within a week, he would turn the newly-revised virus loose in Israel. Once the Jews were dead, he would then turn it loose on targeted inferior races. When he was done, the Fourth Reich would rise again!

~ ~ ~

Dante Schultz was agitated and it showed. It aggravated him that Bern had shown up to take over the operation. Dante was rapidly becoming furious. Senator Bern had put him in charge of this operation. There was no mention of Dieter swooping in to claim credit for the operation. Dante was sure that with Parker's persuasive tactics, Sorenson would have broken and done what was asked of him.

However, Dieter had ordered the scientist killed. Schultz had so far refused to do that. He still felt that Sorenson could prove useful, despite his lack of cooperation so far. He knew that Dieter could order him killed for disobeying a direct order.

That meant that Schultz needed for Sorenson to obey sooner than later. Schultz marched out of his tent and headed for the one where Sorenson was being held. Bern was busy in the lab tent, trying to complete the project that Sorenson had refused to do.

This time, Schultz wouldn't play nice. This time Sorenson was going to understand what true pain was! Schultz grinned as he walked. He would show Dieter Bern who was the true head of Iron Phoenix.

Nick Storm was quietly counting down the numbers in his head. He was locked and loaded and ready to go. He spotted Schultz leaving his tent and heading for the tent where he was certain that Sorenson was being held. "It is time. Fire in the hole," Nick said. Explosions started at each end of the compound as Nick slithered under the fence and moved into a combat crouch and started forward. The numbers were ticking off in his head as slipped unnoticed into the compound while everyone was running around like chickens with their heads cut off.

Schultz was now running for tent where Sorenson was being held, and Nick was hot on his heels. Bodies were dropping as Mac and Jacobs took down enemy combatants. Nick didn't mind, because they were keeping them off of him as he skidded to a halt in front of the tent that Schultz had ducked into. Nick took a breath and let it out slowly. Then, he pushed his way into the tent.

Dante Schultz spun around as Nick Storm stepped inside the tent, his gun at the ready. "Who the hell are you?" Schultz growled.

"Death," Nick replied as he blasted Schultz with the MP-5 Submachine gun. Red blood exploded into the air. Tristan Sorenson looked up at Nick. He was barely recognizable from the beatings that he had received.

"Who the hell are you?" Sorenson said, the words barely audible.

"I'm here to rescue you," Nick told him as he pulled out his knife and severed Sorenson's bonds.

"That doesn't answer my question," Sorenson replied.

"I'm one of the good guys. And I'm getting you out of here. Isn't that good enough?" Nick asked.

"I guess it is," Sorenson sighed.

The pair stepped out of the shack with Storm keeping his H&K at the ready. The camp was in chaos with explosions still going off as munitions cooked off and stray bullets were blasting off in all directions. Nearly dragging Sorenson behind him, Nick headed for the fence line. A pair of soldiers barked at them to stop. Nick spun and dropped to one knee, triggering off a pair of three-round bursts that sent the men to the dirt. He grabbed Sorenson and scrambled towards the fence once more.

~ ~ ~

Dieter Bern was knocked from his feet by the dual explosions. The camp was under attack and that meant the somebody was trying to get the mutated virus. His laptop beeped. The upload of all of Sorenson's research to the thumb drive was complete. Bern grabbed the thumb drive and yanked it free, pausing only to slip it into his pocket. He had what he needed in order to weaponize the virus to a genetically engineered attack. Now, he just had to get it out of the country and to his people so that it could be remanufactured and unleashed on the hated Jews!

~ ~ ~

Mac dropped three more of the Iron Phoenix soldiers before Nick and Sorenson had made it through the fence and into the jungle. Climbing to her feet, Mac began her own ex-fil, heading to the rendezvous point. She assumed that Sean was doing the same.

Sean Jacobs had started his own exfiltration when he spotted Jim King exiting one of the few tents that wasn't on fire. To hell with getting away. He had one job now, and that was to end Jim King's existence. Jacobs ran towards the fencing that surrounded the compound. He slipped inside through the hole he had used to plant the explosives and headed in the direction that Jim King had taken.

~ ~ ~

Jim King was getting the hell out of Dodge. He should never have let the Senator talk him into this crazy-assed job! King wasn't a stary-eyed zealot or patriot, but he wasn't a Nazi either. The money had been damn good while it had lasted, but it meant nothing if he wasn't around to spend it. Two of the Iron Cross soldiers stumbled in front of him. King cut them down without remorse. He didn't even consider them as human, despite the fact that he had been working with them until a few moments ago.

No, he had to get the hell and gone from the camp. Maybe he could still salvage his career at the CIA if he got away quick enough. "King!" a familiar voice cried from behind him. King spun around. A familiar face was charging towards him. "Jacobs?" King asked, not quite believing his eyes.

"Payback is a bitch," Jacobs said as he squeezed the trigger of his assault rifle and held it down. 5.56 tumblers ripped from the barrel of his M-4 and ripped Jim King to shreds. Jacobs ejected the empty mag and rammed a full one home. Now, he could go. Jacobs headed back for the fence and his way home.

~ ~ ~

Sean Jacobs knew that he might well have over-played his hand. Even cutting down Iron Cross soldiers as he made his way to the fence, the chances of him making it out of the compound alive were diminishing with every tick of the clock. Oddly enough, he was now at peace with that. He had avenged his old unit. That was good enough for him.

If he died before he got away, that was okay. He would be at peace with it. Because Jim King was truly dead once and for all. Sean knew that if he died, at least Jim King had preceded him through the gates of hell. That was good enough for him.

~ ~ ~

Nick held the cut in the fence open as Tristan Sorenson scuttled through. Then Nick slipped through behind him. They quickly faded into the underbrush. Nick tapped his com button. "Mac you on the way?"

"Sure thing, Nick. I haven't heard from Sean since everything went boom," Mac replied.

"Shit. Okay, head to the fallback point. I'll see if I can find him," Nick cursed, rolling his eyes. Jacobs was an agent and he knew better than to improvise. If he had not followed orders, he might well be dead. Nick didn't want that on his conscience. No, Sean was not a part of Mac's crew, which meant that he couldn't leave him behind, whether he deserved it or not. He glanced over at Sorenson. "We need to make a slight detour," he sighed.

"What?" Sorenson was looking at him like he was insane.

"Something I learned a long time ago. I don't leave any of my people behind. I've got one missing that went dark right after then excitement got started. We need to find him and determine if he's dead or alive. Of course, if you have a problem with that, you can head back the way we came. Otherwise, shut up and follow me," Nick told him.

~ ~ ~

Washington, D.C.

Jack Riley sat in a van and was watching Senator Bern on surveillance cameras. The Senator had slipped away from his office without his security detail being any the wiser. The only reason a sitting Senator would do that would be if he had something to hide. Riley planned to find out exactly what Bern had to hide.

He had managed to enlist a few pals that had moved into the private security sector to help him bug the Senator's home and office. They had also managed to put a tracker on him as well. That was why Riley was sitting in the van keeping an eye on the man from a distance.

Rick "Ears," Redmond was a specialist in electronic surveillance. Riley had worked with him back in his days with the CIA. Rick had jumped at the chance to help take down a sitting Senator and likely Nazi. Osmond "Ozzy" Frame was an expert in physical surveillance. He was also an old friend that Jack had worked with in the past.

When Riley had called, they had both jumped at the chance to do something other than bust cheating husbands and wives for a change. No, they had both missed the action of working in the covert world.

Senator Bern stepped out of his car. His driver was discreet, and also part of the movement. Bern headed up the sidewalk and into the entryway to the mansion. He rapped on the door three times in rapid succession. A moment later, the door opened and he was ushered inside.

Thirteen

Jack Riley wondered what the Senator was up to. He also wondered who the man was visiting. He would contact Dixon back in Key West. He didn't feel secure using any agency contacts in D.C. Dixon was off the grid at the End of the Road. He was also is contact with Nick and Mac. He texted Dixon the address and asked him to find out who it belonged to.

Jack knew that it might take a while for Dixon to respond, especially if he was busy coordinating things for Nick down in Nicaragua. Jack had a bad feeling about this whole affair. The bad feeling had begun when Jim King had approached Nick to begin with.

~ ~ ~

Nicaragua.

Bullets ripped through the surrounding underbrush, forcing Storm and Sorenson to the ground. Nick rolled over on his back and fired between his feet, hearing screams as he burned through the thirty-round magazine. Quickly, he buttoned out the empty and rammed a full one home and then yanked back the bolt to chamber the top round in the magazine.

Nick rolled to his feet and started moving once again. Sorenson scrambled along behind him. Five minutes later, they hooked up with Jacobs. Nick glared at the CIA agent. "You're late," Nick told him.

"Had some business to take care off," Jacobs replied stoically.

"Uh-huh. That make you risk the whole mission?"

"It was worth it to me. That's all that matters."

"We will talk about this later," Storm told him. Together, the three of them headed for the rendezvous. Nick hoped that Mac had done a better job of following orders than Jacobs had. He had a feeling that he and Jacobs were going to have a heated discussion once they were back on *The Sea Chaser*.

~ ~ ~

Mac was having troubles of her own when she happened on a security patrol that had come running when the heard the explosions from the camp. They were passing right across her path to the rendezvous point. This was the last thing that she needed. Snarling a curse under her breath, Mac reached into the military drop bag hanging from her shoulder. She drew out two old-fashioned pineapple fragmentation grenades. She hooked her thumbs in the rings and used them to pull out the pins. Then she threw them into the knot of soldiers, ducking as they exploded and ripped the group to pieces.

Mac moved down among them, delivering mercy shots into the skulls of the badly wounded survivors. It only took a couple of minutes and then she was on the move again. She had heard other gunfire earlier and wondered if the others had run into trouble.

If they had, Mac was sure that they would be able to handle whatever had come up. Nick was resourceful if nothing else. Still, she worried about Sean Jacobs. He was still new to her crew, acting as a CIA liaison. She didn't know enough about him to trust him yet. She hoped Nick agreed with her.

~ ~ ~

Dieter Bern had escaped from the camp. He had a helicopter stationed a quarter of a mile from the compound. His personal guards were providing security for the chopper while he was at the compound. The Neo-Nazi followed a small path that led from the perimeter of the compound to the clearing. There was still much firing and exploding behind him, that Dieter couldn't tell if the attack was over or not. He didn't really care.

As soon as he appeared in the clearing, his men scrambled to get the chopper ready to lift off. Moving quickly, he entered the helicopter and the pilot started the engine. As the rotors began to turn the engine fired up and within a minute, the chopper lifted into the air.

Bern had a ship waiting on him, an ocean-going yacht with a helipad. Once he reached the yacht, he would take the thumb drive and the virus samples and arrange for a private flight to his laboratory in South Africa. Once there, he would further mutate the virus using gene therapy to vector it toward the Jews.

Iron Phoenix sympathizers in Palestine would receive the mutated virus and unleash it on Israel. His brother would do everything in his power to keep the CDC from sending aid to Israel so that the virus could take hold and then wipe out the Jewish people. Bern smiled at the thought.

~ ~ ~

Mac was waiting when Nick and the others arrived at the rendezvous point. She could tell that Nick wasn't happy, and from the way Sean was acting, she had a feeling that the two had butted heads on the rescue mission. However, this wasn't the time to be asking about it. No, now they needed to get the hell back to the coast and get Sorenson back to the United States.

After pausing for a few minutes to let them catch their breath, Mac took off, taking point on the trail back to the coast. Tristan Sorenson was in bad shape, barely able to walk by himself. That was going to make the exfiltration slower than they needed. They had Sorenson, but that didn't mean that one of the Iron Cross people hadn't managed to escape with the virus.

Mac pulled out her Satellite phone and hit the speed dial for Ezra. "We need a medivac ASAP for Sorenson," Mac said when her first mate answered.

"Send me coordinates and I'll be there as quick as I can get there," Ezra replied. One of *Sea Chaser's* many secrets was the helicopter that was hidden in a compartment on the stern. Ezra had spent time as a rescue pilot during Desert Storm.

"Roger that," Mac replied before texting their coordinates back to the boat.

~ ~ ~

Dieter Bern was anxious. Things were starting to move fast, faster than he had anticipated. However, despite that, his plan was coming together. Iron Phoenix had infiltrated both government and the Military in Germany. Once the Valhalla virus was released in the Middle East and started killing off the Jews, Bern and his Iron Cross allies in Germany would over-through the government and the Fourth Reich would rise like a phoenix from the ashes of the Third Reich.

~ ~ ~

Ezra King flew the helicopter skimming the tree tops as he headed for the coordinates that Mac had sent him. The chopper was a Viet Nam era UH 1 Iroquois that had been refitted and repurposed for covert operations for *The Sea Chaser*. Fiona was riding along because she was an experienced medic as well as being the ship's engineer.

"How much longer?" Fiona asked via her headset.

"Three, maybe four minutes," Ezra replied.

"I can hear you coming, popping green smoke to guide you in," Mac's voice sounded in their ears. Suddenly, a column of green smoke lifted into the air from a clearing ahead of them.

"We see you, and we'll be right there," Ezra replied, guiding the chopper in over the clearing and settling the whirly-bird to the ground. Mac and the others dragged Tristan Sorenson to the Chopper and they all got aboard. Ezra lifted the bird into the air and headed back towards the boat.

~ ~ ~

Washington, D.C.

"Who owns this place?" Ears Redmond asked as they followed Senator Bern to a large mansion just off the Washington beltway.

"That's what I hired you guys to find out," Riley rolled his eyes.

"I knew there had to be a reason," Ears chuckled.

"If you guys need to be somewhere else," Ozzy Frame suggested.

"I think he's trying to get rid of us," Ears chuckled.

"I wonder why," Riley huffed. It wasn't really a question. And Jack knew that Ozzy was only kidding. The three of them enjoyed the kind of comradery that came from serving together under fire on the battlefield in many of the hell grounds around the globe. Jack had worked with them as part of a counter-terrorism team back in his CIA days before he had quit to become a Chicago cop. He shook the memory away before the more painful ones came up of his deceased wife and his deceased best friend and former partner on the force. Those he kept locked up tight in a box that he never wanted to open again.

"Give me a couple of minutes and I can find out," Ozzy said, working the computer keyboard in front of him. Ears was busy setting of a laser beam to bounce of the lighted window upstairs so they could listen in on whatever was being said inside the room.

"Get me what you can," Jack told him.

"Roger that," Ozzy replied.

~ ~ ~

Nicaragua.

Mac and Gina loaded Sorenson onto a gurney that they had on-board for medical emergencies and started pushing him toward the medical bay. Gina had medical training as did Mac, so the medical care of the scientist would be in their capable hands. Nick, Sean, Fiona, and Ezra tied the chopper back down and lowered it below deck on a mechanical platform and then closed the hidden hatch. Nick looked at Sean. "We need to talk," Nick told him. Sensing the tension between the two, Fiona and Ezra made themselves scarce.

"What?" Sean asked, more than a little belligerently.

"What part of the orders I gave you did you not understand," Nick asked softly.

"Jim King is dead. So, as far as I'm concerned, the mission was a total success," Sean shrugged.

"Smack!" Nick enjoyed the sound of his fist smashing into Sean Jacobs face. The CIA liaison fell backward onto the deck. His face red and angry, the Agency man jumped to his feet, but Nick hit him again and then kicked his knee out from under him. Sean Jacobs screamed as he fell to the deck, clutching his injured knee.

"We will never speak of this again," Nick told him before walking off, leaving the injured man squirming on the deck. Sean shot daggers after Storm. If looks could kill, Nick Storm would already be dead.

As Nick walked towards the bridge. Ezra King appeared from nowhere. Ezra paused to help Sean off the deck. "Whatever you did, it wasn't smart. It doesn't pay to piss Nick Storm off," Ezra told him.

"I don't really give a shit. I owe the bastard one and I plan to collect," Sean snarled.

"Then I hope your life insurance is paid off," Ezra replied, meaning every word.

~ ~ ~

Fiona was at the bridge when Nick entered. She gave him a smile, but it didn't seem to faze him. Fiona frowned. Not being noticed by men was *not* something that she was used to. She found it frustrating that Nick Storm never seemed to notice her when he was aboard. Part of it, she knew, was that he still had feelings for Mac. And while Mac was her friend, Fiona liked Nick Storm and wanted him for herself. She hoped that it wouldn't be too much of a problem. She had been working for Mac for a long time and they were the best of friends. However, all was fair in love and war.

Nick walked over and asked if Mac was still in the Medical Bay. Fiona said she was, and watched as Nick Storm headed below deck. She sighed. Why was it that all of the good men always had a lot of unpacked baggage?

~ ~ ~

Mac and Gina had hooked Sorenson up to an IV and had loaded it up with pain medication and antibiotics. Sorenson moaned softly. He was still unconscious. Mac gave him a sedative to ensure that he would stay that way for the next few hours. The scientist was in bad shape. They needed him alive so that he might help stop whatever Iron Cross had in mind.

"How's he looking?" Nick asked as he entered the Medical Bay.

'I think he'll live," Gina told him. Nick nodded and gave Mac a look. She followed him back up to the main deck.

"What?" Mac asked.

"Sean disobeyed orders and did a little off-mission work. It needed to be done, but he put us all at risk. That is a problem," Nick told her.

"I have no control over Sean, he was appointed to be our liaison by the CIA. I can request that he be removed, but that is the best I can do," Mac replied.

"I figured that. I just thought that you should be aware of the problem," Nick explained.

"I know. You do know that Fiona is interested in you?"

"I know."

"Don't hurt her, Nick."

"I won't," Nick promised.

~ ~ ~

Washington, D.C.

Jack and Ears stayed on the Senator while Oz settled in to follow the person that Senator Bern had met with. A quick search of some restricted data bases gave him a name and photograph. Edgar Klausen was listed at the home owner. Ozzy texted that information to Riley who in turn sent it to Dixon so the cyber-specialist could do a deep dive on the man.

Ozzy had decided to get proactive and plant trackers on Klausen's two vehicles, one a black SUV and the other a Navy-colored Porsche. Static surveillance is not the easiest choice to make. But with the GPS trackers in place, he was positioned where he could track the man remotely if he left in either of the two vehicles that belonged with him.

Ozzy and Ears had opened their own private security service after leaving the CIA. They worked well together. Picking up bonus jobs like this one for Riley was just icing on the cake for the pair. It also gave them a chance to revisit the hell grounds where they had originally formed their bond.

Fourteen

Edgar Klausen left the house shortly after Senator Bern. That was what Ozzy had been waiting for. He let Klausen get a block away before starting the motor of his gray Chevy Impala, the body was a decade old but the motor was supercharged with turbo-engine. If it looked like Klausen might get away, Ozzy was very confident that he would be able to catch the man fairly quickly.

~ ~ ~

Nicaragua, Central America.

"Bern escaped, so what do we do now?" Sean Jacobs asked, shooting a dirty look at Nick. Storm ignored him as he considered their next move.

"We need to catch up to Bern. Mac, can Ezra fly us to Aeropuerto nacional? I can make arrangements with Dixon for Jay Barn to pick us up there and go after Bern," Nick sighed. Mac glanced over at Ezra and saw him give a nod.

"Make the call," Mac told him. Ezra left the room and began to refuel and pre-flight the chopper. She then looked at Storm. "Let's go prepare for our journey."

"Roger that," Nick replied, following her out of the conference room. They stopped by the armory to pick out what they might need. Nick picked up a pair of MP-5 Sub Machineguns and six extra magazines for both. He also added six extra magazines for his S&W M&P Shield single stack .45. Mac had loaded her go bag with extra magazines and ammunition for her Ruger SC9 and both gas and flash bangs. She added a couple of fragmentation grenades for good measure. They both grabbed a change of clothes in case they had to go out into the city. The tiger-stripe BDU's they were wearing would look out of place in the city.

"Do we know where Bern is headed?" Mac asked.

"Not exactly, but I have a good idea. I had Dixon do some digging," Nick replied.

"Getting ahead of things?"

"Trying. This virus is deadly and the last thing we need is for it to get out into the world."

"Do you really think Iron Cross is stupid enough to do that?"

"They are Nazis after all," Nick shook his head.

"That scares me, Nick." Mac sighed.

"It should. Those fools are liable to do anything."

"World War Two proved that."

"Yes, it did."

Twenty minutes later, they were in the chopper and Ezra was ferrying them across country to the nearest airport. Nick used a radio link to update Dixon and to see what he had on Bern's movements.

~ ~ ~

Fiona frowned as she watched Sean Jacobs. He was in a bit of a funk. He looked positively furious as he watched the chopper head off over the jungle. "What's got your panties in a twist?" she asked.

"I hate that fucker," Sean growled.

"Can you be more specific?"

"Nick Storm. I owe that bastard for the way he treated me."

"Sean, you need to let it go. You are only here because Mac gave her okay. You try anything with Nick and you very well might get tossed overboard in the middle of the ocean," Fiona replied.

"I really don't care," Sean replied. Fiona rolled her eyes. Of course, he would say that now with neither Mac of Nick on board. The likelihood of him saying that if either of them were in the room was little to none.

"Haul up the anchor. We need to head back to the Panama Canal and head for the Atlantic Ocean," Fiona told him. Sean gave her a surly look and went to do as she ordered.

Fiona frowned. Sean was rapidly turning into a problem. She hoped that Mac would deal with it when they got back to the Atlantic side of the Panama Canal.

Fiona offered up a prayer to King Neptune that they would make it back okay,

Ezra dropped them off on the shores of the Atlantic. Nick and Mac picked up a car that had been left for them by a friend of Dixon's. "Are you sure about this?" Mac asked as Nick pulled the vehicle onto the road. They were headed for Managua, because it seemed the most likely place that Iron Cross might have a safehouse.

"No, I'm not. Right now, I'm not sure about anything on this mission, other than we need to stop Iron Cross from releasing that virus." Nick replied. "Jim King brought me into what I am pretty sure was an unsanctioned mission, figuring if I blew it, he had a scapegoat in me to put the blame on. He didn't count on me figuring out what he was up to. Sean took King out over a blown mission a few years back, effectively removing King from the equation. Now it is just us against Iron Cross."

"So where to now?" Mac asked.

"I figure Bern will try to fly out of the country so Dixon put a team in place there to watch for him. I'm betting he will try to leave the country by boat, and then grab a flight from one of the Caribbean islands," Storm replied.

~ ~ ~

Washington, D.C.

Ozzy Frame had done a Nexus/Lexis search on Edgar Klausen. The man was a German national who had immigrated to the United States in the late 1950's. He brought with him a lot of money and within a decade was a well-known industrialist, building factories that built everything from automobiles to planes and tanks for the Department of Defense. He had provided DARPA with funds to experiment with new types of weapons.

It hadn't taken him long to become part of the Washington social scene. He became an indispensable advisor to congressmen and senators. His campaign contributions had helped instill many of them in their political seats. Edgar Klausen was also a former Nazi who had buried his past behind him with a veneer of respectability.

As Ozzy watched, a car was brought around and Klausen exited from the mansion, followed by two men that Frame could only assume were his bodyguards. The trio entered the car and pulled out of the drive. Frame started his own vehicle and pulled out into the street, following from about half a block away.

~ ~ ~

Ears and Jack followed the Senator's vehicle back to his office and watched as Bern went back inside. "I wonder what that was all about?"

"Maybe we can still find out," Ears said as he opened a hard plastic case and removed a drone and its controller.

"What do you have in mind?" Riley asked, watching his friend prepare the drone to fly. He had spotted the camera and a small green dot laser mounted on the device.

"How about we listen to what the Senator has on his mind after his trip?" Ears grinned.

"That sounds suspiciously like a plan. The more information we have, the easier to put Senator Blake Bern's head in a noose," Riley grinned back.

~ ~ ~

Managua, Nicaragua.

Gina Torres had spent the past few hours working on Tristan Sorenson and his various bruises and cracked ribs. "You look like hell, Tristan," Gina told him.

"But I can still tap dance," Sorenson groaned.

"I pretty much doubt that," Gina rolled her eyes.

"How soon before you can get me back to the States?"

"According to my friends, a private operator will be in touch with us soon. Then it is as simple as going to the airport," Gina shrugged.

"It's never that simple," Sorenson groaned.

"Hopefully, this time it is," Gina replied.

~ ~ ~

Nick and Mac headed for the port. Rather than risk a direct plane out of Managua, Nick was fairly certain that Bern would try to leave the country via boat, preferably one big enough to land a helicopter on once it was out at sea and far away from the coast. Bern would not want anyone to know exactly how he made his escape. Disappearing in the middle of the ocean would only enhance his already burgeoning reputation.

Iron Phoenix was rapidly becoming a rising star in the world of International Terrorism. They were known to help spread money and influence to help the Neo-Nazi organizations grow across the world. Now that they had this new bio-weapon to threaten their enemies with, Iron Phoenix had to be stopped, and Nick knew that it was his job to get it done. Sure, he had Mac along for the ride to help him, but it was his job to stop Bern and his minions from unleashing Valhalla on an unsuspecting world.

Nick and Mac split up when they reached the port. They were on coms and Mac had a better idea of what to look for in private crafts, leaving Nick with the larger cargo ships and steamers.

It was mid-afternoon and the docks were busy. Cargo cranes lifting containers from ships, while others placed new containers on them. Sailors and longshore men bustled about. Nick did his best to blend in as he searched for some sign of Dieter Bern and his Neo-Nazi buddies.

~ ~ ~

Mac made her way towards the public docks where the rich and privileged kept their playthings. She was good at reading the nuances of the rich and infamous. She had almost been one of them herself. That was a long time ago. Longer than she cared to think about. Having been born to money and privilege, Mac was at home among the rich and shameless. She could also spot the wannabes. It didn't take her long to locate Dieter Bern's boat. Mac pulled out her phone and dialed Nick's number.

Nick joined her in less than five minutes, and they had taken up a position where they could easily observe the boat and the gangplank leading to its deck. Mac had already spotted Bern when he had arrived and they knew that he was on board. The question was for how long?

Nick placed a quick call to Larry Dixon and let him know that they had located Bern. Dixon pulled the surveillance from the airport and put in a call to Jay Barr to be available on a moment's notice. Dixon was pretty sure that Nick would be ready to jump once Bern was in motion.

"So, what do we do now?" Mac asked.

"Now, we wait," Nick replied.

Surveillance is one of the least rewarding parts of being a spy. It is long, it is boring. You do nothing but sit and wait for something to happen. It goes better with a second person to help keep you alert and spell you when nature calls. Mac and Storm had been at it for the past three hours. So far, there had been no sign of Dieter Bern. So, where the hell was, he? Had he faked them all out and slipped out of the country by another route all together?

"Dammit!' Nick stood and began to pace. He hated waiting for something to happen. He was more of a direct-action type of guy and had been since his days with the CIA's Special Activities Group. Of course, that was long ago, but he still felt that sense of frustration and impatience.

"You haven't changed all that much, Nick Storm," Mac told him.

"Maybe not. I still hate this part of the job."

"Well, you can relax. Our target just arrived," Mac told him.

"I wonder where he's been?" Nick picked up binoculars and focused them on the boat.

"If I had to guess, I'd say that he stopped to work on the virus," Mac replied.

"You're probably right. How long do you think they will stay in port?"

"I'd say not long."

"Call Jay and tell him to pick us up."

"Copy that," Mac replied as she picked up her cell and dialed the pilot. Nick was busy watching the crew of the yacht start untying and throwing off lines. He could hear the rumble as the engines came to life. It started moving out away from the docks.

"Shit!" Nick exclaimed, dropping the binoculars and taking off at a run. He wasn't sure exactly what he was going to do. He hadn't thought that far ahead. But he had to do something, so he was racing along the pier as the yacht edged away from the dock. Five feet. Ten feet. Nick launched himself off the dock towards the yacht's fantail.

Stretching with every ounce of his being, Nick hooked his fingers over the edge of the fantail. His body slammed into the rear bulkhead with enough force to knock the wind out of him. Nick gasped for air as he dangled off the back of the yacht, then he slowly pulled himself up and over. But now that he was on the boat, how was he going to hide until he could make a move on either Dieter Bern or the cannister filled with the weaponized virus.

Glancing around, he scrambled up onto the roof of the pilothouse where he could hide among the radar and communications gear situated up there. The yacht was now out into the bay and heading for open water. Nick hoped that Mac had gotten ahold of Jay Barr. Without the pilot and the helicopter, this might just be a one-way trip for Storm.

Mac had watched Storm make his impulsive race to get on the yacht and was cursing under breath while her cell-phone was ringing. "Yeah?" Jay Barr growled in her ear.

"This Mac, I need an immediate pick up at the docks here. You know where."

"Give me ten minutes. Where's Storm?"

"You wouldn't believe me if I told you," Mac replied, breaking the connection.

Fifteen

Storm was already regretting his impulsive race to board the departing yacht. The roof was painted white and reflected both sunlight and heat into him. The radar and communications gear did not provide a lot in the way of shade and he had no water with him. All he had was a pistol, two spare magazines and his knife. And a pack of chewing gum. That might come in handy to keep him salivating. Hydration was going to be a problem.

Unless it started to rain. That was a whole bunch of other problems, but at least he wouldn't die of dehydration. Nick mentally kicked himself. It was this sort of wild-ass impulsiveness that had gotten him into trouble during his days with the CIA. Hopefully Mac had gotten Jay Barr and she and the master Caribe pilot were in the air and tracking him.

If not, well then, he was going to be royally fucked! Storm closed his eyes for a brief moment, trying to decide what to do next. He could try to take over the yacht, but he had no idea how many people he was up against on the yacht. No, he had a feeling if he did that it would not end well. So, what did that leave him? Nowhere for at least the moment.

~ ~ ~

Mac and Barr were in the air within seconds of his landing at the port parking lot, and then they were swinging back out over the bay heading for open sea. Mac knew that they had to find Storm and do it quickly. The impulsive former Caribe agent was in more danger than even he realized. Word had just come in from Dixon that Bern had indeed mutated the virus and it was now totally weaponized.

Mac was using her binoculars to scan the ocean below, searching for the yacht that Storm had boarded. Thanks to Larry Dixon and Jack Riley, the United States Navy was also involved in searching for the yacht. However, Mac knew that she needed to find it first while Nick was still alive. Because if they took too long to find him, she was sure that he would die.

~ ~ ~

Dieter Bern frowned. Something was wrong, but he wasn't sure what it was. He had felt it when they had left the port behind them. It was really nothing more than a hidden itch on the back of his neck. However, Bern had not risen to the leadership of Iron Phoenix by ignoring such feelings.

Bern locked the cannister containing the virus in a small safe aboard the boat. Then, drawing his pistol, Bern headed out to search for whatever was bothering him. It was likely that the American agents were on his trail, trying to stop his mission. They would have to be stopped of course. Valhalla must be unleashed first in Israel and then on America! Then the world would bow to the Fourth Reich and Iron Phoenix!

~ ~ ~

"Can you see them yet?" Barr asked as he sent the Vietnam era Huey climbing out over the bay.

"Not yet," Mac replied. She had moved into the crew section and loaded up the chain gun. She had a feeling that they might well need the firepower. Not for the first time, she cursed Nick's impulsiveness under her breath. They had to get Nick back and stop Bern, however both did not need to happen at the same time. "There!" Mac shouted, pointing to the left. Jay followed her pointing arm and spotted the yacht.

Jay Barr put the chopper into a deep dive, pulling up at the last moment as the rotors flared. Mac picked that moment to fire at the yacht, cutting down three men that had run out of the pilot house. Barr spotted Storm as he dropped down to the deck, pistol in his hand.

Gunfire erupted from the pilothouse, sending splinters of fiberglass and wood spraying at the American agent. Storm spun and dropped to one knee, firing back at the shooter inside. Then, Storm was up and running towards the rear of the boat. He launched himself into the air and splashed down into the clear blue waters of the bay.

The yacht accelerated away from the area and headed for open sea while Barr spun the chopper around and dropped down to wave-top level so that Storm could reach the landing skid and pull himself aboard.

~ ~ ~

Washington, D.C.
Ozzy Frame followed Edgar Klausen away from the beltway and into suburban Virginia. Frame was able to hang back about half a mile and follow them using the trackers he had placed on Klausen's vehicles. That proved to be a good thing when Klausen turned into the drive of a gated property. Ozzy drove on past and parked a way down the twisting road.

Riley hadn't asked for him to go EVA on the job, but Ozzy had prepared to do so anyway. Grabbing a loaded M-4 assault rifle from the back seat, and taking some laser surveillance gear. Ozzy went in search of a point where he could see and hopefully hear what was going on in the house where Klausen had gone.

Ozzy had been blooded during Operation Desert Storm as part of the special forces ground assault team that had been slipped in behind enemy lines. He and Ears and worked together. And that was where they had first met Jack Riley. The three of them had bonded during that conflict, and the bond had lasted far beyond it. That was why he was sneaking through the dense forest of suburban Virginia.

Klausen had connections to the Neo-Nazi group known as Iron Phoenix. It was very possible that he was the go between for Blake Bern and his son Dieter. That meant that he might have information about whatever Dieter Bern might have planned.

~ ~ ~

The Caribbean Sea.

"We've lost them," Jay Barr said with a disgusted sigh.

"That sucks," Nick admitted.

"So, what now?" Mac asked, looking from one to the other.

"It means I drop you off at the nearest military base and you do what Riley tells you to do," Barr replied.

"I can live with that," Nick told him.

~ ~ ~

Gina Torres was watching over him when Tristan Sorenson regained consciousness. "Hey, Boss you finally decide to get up?" she asked with a grin.

"Gina? How, where am I? What happened? Sorenson struggled to sit up. Gina easily pushed him back down.

"Slow down, Hoss. Give me a minute and I'll lay it all out for you," Gina told him.

"You were kidnapped by terrorists. I met up with a couple of people that rescued you. Now they are chasing down said terrorists to stop them from using the virus," she explained.

"How did you get here?"

"Well, the guy that came looking for you, rescued me from Iron Cross, that's the terrorist group, and then he helped get you out of their camp. Now Nick Storm and Mac Mackenzie are chasing a dude named Dieter Bern before he can unleash the virus you weaponized," Gina explained.

"Gina, I need to get back to the States right away. I can help the CDC neutralize the virus before it takes hold. Can your friends make that happen?"

"All I can do is ask. However, given how dangerous Valhalla is in its weaponized form, I'm betting they can make it happen," Gina replied. "Rest here and I'll go find out."

"I can do that," Sorenson nodded, closing his eyes.

~ ~ ~

Fiona looked up when Gina Torres entered the pilothouse. "How is our patient?" Fiona asked.

"Doing better. He says that if we can get him back to the United States in time that he can help neutralize the weaponized virus. Can you help with that?" Gina asked.

"Let me make a few calls," Fiona replied.

"I can't let you do that," Sean Jacob's voice carried an air of menace. The two women looked at him and were shocked to see that he was pointing a submachine gun at them.

"Sean, what the hell are you doing?" Fiona asked, her Irish accent deepening from stress.

"My job. You see, my first allegiance isn't to the CIA and America at all. No, my allegiance is to the Motherland and Iron Cross. Knowing that the virus has been weaponized means that Bern has succeeded. It will be unleashed on the world and soon, the Fourth Reich will rise from the ashes and the Master Race will rule the world!" Sean smiled, it was a smile without humor and disturbing to look at.

"You can't be serious."

"I'm dead serious. All that remains is for me to eliminate everyone on this boat and then disappear. It's not so far to Argentina and many members of the Reich still hold power there."

"Do you really think you can get away with this?" Fiona asked, moving to her left. As Jacobs' eyes followed her, she could see Gina moving to her right, creating more space between them. From what Mac had told her, Torres could hold her own in a fight. However, Fiona planned to even the odds as much as she could.

"I wouldn't be here if I didn't. I hope you ladies are prepared to die," Sean Jacobs smiled. Just then something slammed into the back of his neck, pitching him forward. He managed to trigger off a burst from the MP-5, but failed to hit anyone. Ezra kicked him in the back of the head while Fiona arrived and tore the gun from his grasp.

Ezra pulled out a pair of plastic ties and used them to temporarily bind his hands. One thing that Sean Jacobs had forgotten was that Mac kept actual irons for problems like this. The flexicuffs would be cut once the physical irons had been locked around Jacobs' wrists.

"What now?" Gina asked.

"Now I get you and Dr. Sorenson a ride back to the States," Fiona replied.

"I'll go let Tristan know," Gina smiled.

"You do that. Get him ready to travel," Fiona replied as she reached for the satellite phone.

~ ~ ~

Nick and Mac had been deposited on an aircraft carrier that was moving towards the Caribbean from Panama. Nick had contacted Jack Riley for instructions. Mac watched his face as he received his orders. He didn't look happy at what he was hearing. He hung up with a sigh.

"Well?" Mac asked.

"The news isn't good. Bern has managed to disappear, along with Valhalla."

"Do we have any idea where he might have disappeared to?"

"Maybe, Haiti, maybe Jamacia," Stone shrugged.

"So, what do we do now?"

"Haiti is closer, so we go there and catch a flight to Israel. That seems to be the most likely target for Iron Phoenix."

"So, we are going to work with Mossad?" Mac asked.

"It looks like it."

"Israel is a long way from the Caribbean.

"So, it appears to be."

"Can you operate over there?" Mac asked.

"I can. For the moment, I'm doing contract work for the CIA. I can operate anywhere outside the United States," Storm grinned.

"So, what now?" Mac asked.

"We grab a flight to Israel," Storm replied with a grin.

Sixteen

"Riley," Jack answered his cell.

"Bern was meeting with Edgar Klausen. Klausen just arrived at an Iron Phoenix owned property in Baltimore. The guards on the gate greeted him like he was an old friend before they let him in," Ozzy replied.

"Are you getting it on video?"

"Do you really need to ask?"

"I suppose not. I'm gonna leave Ears on Bern and I'll join you. Text me the address," Riley commanded. He had already contacted his liaison at the Department of Justice for a ride and a SWAT team made up of United States Deputy Marshals.

~ ~ ~

Dominican Republic, La Romana International Airport.

Dieter Bern was already on board a plane taking off from the airport when Storm and Mac arrived. Their trip had been delayed while Larry Dixon was cutting through bureaucratic red tape on Riley's orders. From the DR, they would catch a plane to Europe and then a plane to Israel where they would meet up with a Mossad agent with the code name of Moses.

The airwaves were burning between Langley and Tel Aviv as the two governments began to work together. Mac looked over at Storm as they sat reading newspapers to kill time before their flight boarded. "What is on your mind, Nick?" Mac asked.

"Jack is working the D.C. angle and they are closing in on the Iron Cross cell there. Our job is to catch Dieter and keep him from unleashing that virus in Israel," Nick replied.

"How do you think he will do that?"

"That's what we have to figure out," Nick told her. The pair put their heads together, trying to figure out a plan until they were called to board their plane to Europe. Hopefully, by the time they arrived in Israel, they would have a plan.

~ ~ ~

Tel Aviv.

Ari Feldman, *codename Moses* was waiting when the plane carrying the two American CIA agents arrived at the terminal. Ari was tall and powerfully built, with curly black hair and soulful brown eyes that made him a hit with the ladies. He had been chosen to work with the American agents to hunt down this Dieter Bern and his weaponized virus. Already, specially equipped teams armed with hazmat and anti-viral cleaning agents had been mobilized and located at potential target sites. Ari hoped that the two agents could give him some into this terrorist's mind. How he thought, how he planned.

Ari was dressed in a white tropical linen suit with dark shoes. His shirt was light blue. Beneath his jacket he carried a Beretta PX4 Storm 9mm in a shoulder holster and four spare magazines, two under his arm and two on his belt. He had studied photos of the two American agents so that he could easily spot them when they got off the plane.

The pair almost looked like they had come out of central casting for an action movie. Nick Storm was well-built and muscular, a handsome face, dark hair streaked with blond high-lights. He wore Khaki cargo pants, a pale blue shirt and brown desert combat boots. Dark sunglasses covered his eyes. The girl was a thin blond that curved in all of the right places. She moved with the rolling gait of someone who spent a lot of time on boats, which fit with the dossiers that had been sent on them.

Ari followed the pair after they cleared customs. He waited until they paused at a news stand to grab a newspaper to make his approach. "Did you really part the Red Sea?" Nick Storm asked softly as he pivoted to face Ari.

"Not lately. But who knows what may carry us to the halls of Valhalla?" Ari replied, giving the proper response code. The two men shook hands as Mac watched. "What now?"

"Take us someplace where we can talk that isn't so public," Nick replied.

"I can do that," Ari told him. The pair picked up their carry-on luggage and followed him out to the parking garage.

~ ~ ~

Tel Aviv is a coastal town on the Mediterranean and one of the most populated cities in the Jewish State. It had been easy enough for Dieter Bern to vanish after he had left his plane. Iron Phoenix had actually established several safehouses across the city. Bern headed for one of them. For the moment, the vaunted Mossad had no idea that the Neo-Nazi group had managed to infiltrate their country.

Franz Guttenbaum had been a sleeper agent among the Jews since shortly after the Six-Day War. He was known and respected as businessman and banker in Tel Aviv. As one of the political elite, Guttenbaum had a line into the current government as well as connections to the intelligence community. This plan had been set in motion shortly after World War II.

Guttenbaum was old and thin with a wispy cap of white hair that resembled cotton fluff. His eyebrows were still dark and bushy, but they only seemed to accent his cold dark eyes. "The iron Phoenix rises from the flames of the past," Guttenbaum said/

"To be reborn in the future from the flames of the past," Bern replied, completing the password. The two men shook hands and Guttenbaum escorted the Neo-Nazi scientist inside his home.

"I need to test the virus," Bern told the old man.

"How do you want to do that?"

"I have a small aerosol delivery system. I want to send someone on a bus to release the virus so we can make sure it works as we were told it would," Bern replied.

"We can make that happen," Guttenbaum told him.

"Good. I am certain of my results, but I want to test them to be sure. The Fourth Reich will rise from the ashes, and Iron Phoenix to rule the world!" Bern replied.

~ ~ ~

Marvin and his bride of thirty years Norma Leeds had come to visit the Holy land because that was where their ancestors had come from. Marvin was in his sixties with fluffy cotton white hair and a sun burned face. Norma was a petite woman, barely five feet tall. Her white hair was thinning.

They were walking through an open-air market looking for trinkets to purchase to take home to their grandkids back in New York City. It was a bright and sunny day, much the norm for the Israeli capital city. Despite that fact that most of the Middle Eastern countries around them wanted to destroy them, the Israeli people took it in stride. They had one of the top intelligence agencies in the world. So, most tourists travelled in the capitol city without fear.

Marvin and Norma were no different. They felt a spritz of moisture as they passed an open-air stand. Neither of them thought anything of it. Not until they were twenty yards beyond the stall. Suddenly both began to cough and gasp for air as they staggered and collapsed to the ground. Blood began to pour from their eyes, nose, and mouths. A policeman's whistle began to shrill as on-lookers used their cellular phones to record the chaos that was breaking out as other people began to collapse.

Ari Feldman answered his cellphone but his expression quickly darkened as he listened to the caller. Nick Storm figured that the news he was getting wasn't good based on how the Mossad agent tensed up the longer he listened. Storm stepped in front of the man. "What is it?" Storm asked.

"There has been a terrorist attack here in the city. Several people are dead or dying from what appears to be a weaponized biological attack," Ari replied.

"Valhalla," Storm whispered.

"It seems so. Come with me," Ari ordered, heading for a dark SUV parked nearby. Mac and Storm followed along. This was the reason why they were in Israel, to find Bern and stop the spread of the Valhalla virus.

"Can you tell us what exactly happened?" Storm asked as he settled back into the passenger seat. Mac had climbed into the back so she could both keep and eye on Ari and on their back trail. Nobody seemed to be following them as Ari sped towards the coastal part of the city.

"Several people were at an open-air market, when they felt what they were water droplets from a hydration fan. Except they weren't. Within seconds, people started coughing and gasping for air. Then they collapsed and started vomiting. Blood began to leak from their eyes, ears and mouth. The market has been closed and is being decontaminated after the incident. This disease is not only deadly, but it strikes very fast," Ari revealed.

"That sounds like the Valhalla virus to me," Nick sighed.

"It sure does. Our people have the scientist that weaponized it in custody and he is currently working to create a cure," Mac added.

"You might have mentioned it sooner," Ari rolled his eyes as he drove.

"No, she loves to surprise people," Nick shook his head.

"A girl has to have her fun where she can find it," Mac grinned.

"Americans," Ari grunted in aggravation.

~ ~ ~

Medical personnel in white hazmat suits were checking bodies as well as searching for however the virus had been dispersed. Ari got them as close as he could while still staying outside of the quarantine zone which was marked off with strips of yellow caution tape.

"Is this what you expected?" Ari asked.

"No, it is worse," Nick sighed. "I need to contact Langley."

"We will go to my safe house then. It has its own special classified containment communications room where you can speak without worry of you call being intercepted. I just hope that you will brief me afterward of what you find out."

"I can do that," Storm told him.

"I need to call *The Sea Chaser* and check on my crew as well," Mac added. Nick nodded. He also wanted to know what was going on back on the boat. Mac apparently knew that Sorenson was in United States Custody by now. While he hadn't checked in with Dixon, Nick believed Mac. That meant that something had gone wrong aboard *The Sea Chaser*. Nick also needed to know what had happened.

~ ~ ~

Pacific Ocean, north of Panama.

Fiona answered the satellite phone when it rang. She knew that it was Mac on the other end of the line and this was a conversation that she really didn't want to have, figuring that she really didn't need an ass chewing. However, there was no way around it, so she answered the call. "*Sea Chaser*, Fiona speaking."

"Awfully formal, Fi. Tell me what is going on," Mac ordered.

"We had an incident."

"What kind of incident?"

"A fatal one."

"Quit beating around the bush and tell me what happened." Mac's voice was cold and hard. Fiona winced at the tone.

"Our CIA pal tried to kill Sorenson. It seems he was actually a mole for Iron Phoenix," Fiona sighed.

"And?" Mac inquired. Fiona was glad she was out of her captain's physical reach.

"Ezra had to take him out before he killed Sorenson. After that, I called Dixon and had him arrange emergency transport for Gina and Sorenson back to the United States. We gave the traitor a burial at sea." Fiona explained.

"Glad that is taken care of, but I'll have to make nice with Langley to make sure we are forgiven and not sanctioned for taking the mole out," Mac sighed.

"Sorry, Boss. It was the only way to keep Dr. Sorenson alive," Fiona said softly, her voice barely above a whisper.

"Don't worry about it. Nick and Jack Riley will help smooth things out," Mac told her before breaking the connection.

~ ~ ~

Tel Aviv.

"Bad news?" Nick asked. He could tell from her body language the Meredith Mackenzie was not happy with what she had just learned.

"Sean Jacobs is dead. It appears that he was a mole for Iron Phoenix. He tried to kill Sorenson, but Ezra took him out before he could. I made need some help from your boss to smooth that out."

"He will help," Nick assured her.

"I figured. The good news is that Sorenson and Miss Torres are already in Atlanta with the CDC working on a cure," Mac told him.

"That is good news. I had a feeling about Sean. Something about him never rang true, especially when he went rogue in Nicaragua when we were breaking Sorenson out of the Iron Phoenix base camp," Storm told her.

"Your feeling was correct. Why don't you call Dixon and see if he can get us an update on that antidote?" Mas asked.

"Good idea. It will up our stock with the Israelis," Nick replied pulling out his phone. He pulled up his contacts and called the emergency number for the Caribe headquarters.

~ ~ ~

Dieter Bern smiled as he watched the news reports. The sudden deaths at the market from a mystery virus with symptoms similar to Ebola was the top story of the hour. People were being ordered to go home and shelter in place so that this mystery virus didn't spread.

Seventeen

Tristan Sorenson swore as he listened to the news reports from Israel on Fox News. His greatest fear had been realized and Valhalla had been released in Tel Aviv. He recognized it had only been a small dispersal or the casualties would be much worse. Sorenson cursed under his breath as he worked to reverse engineer a cure. Gina Torres was in the lab beside him. So far, her help had been invaluable.

She had worked with him to engineer Valhalla, so it was only fitting that she worked beside him to create a cure. They also had every single virologist in the CDC working with them, most following his lead.

Sorenson yawned loudly, then paused to rub his eyes. He was tired, still not having a chance to rest since his arrival in Atlanta. Jet lag was murder! He felt a hand on his shoulder. It was Gina. "You need to rest or you won't be able to end this scourge. If you are worn out, your mind is not as sharp and you are not your best self."

"I know, but I'm not sure I can afford to take the time to rest," Tristan replied soberly.

"You have to. At the least take a nap. Two hours won't mean the end of the world."

"You hope," Tristan yawned once more. Finally, Tristan let her lead him out of the lab to a room with a bed in it. Sorenson's eyes closed and he was asleep before his head hit the pillow. Gina yawned as well, but then she turned and headed back to the lab to continue her efforts to find a cure.

She knew that Tristan felt guilty about what he had been tricked into doing. Gina would do whatever she could to help him stop the chimera that he had created. Gina wondered if Storm and Mackenzie were making any progress in tracking down the man that had taken the virus.

~ ~ ~

Washington, D.C.

Ozzy had parked a block away from Klausen's home. He was using a drone to get a better layout of the place while he waited for Riley and the U.S. Marshals to arrive. He slipped his own weapon out of the leather beneath his left arm, checking to make sure he had a live round in the chamber just in case it was needed.

Ozzy checked his watch. Riley and the Marshals should be arriving soon. Hopefully they wouldn't be walking into an ambush when they got there. Iron Phoenix had a reputation for terror and brutality. If Klausen was a major player in the terrorism game, then it was possible that they might be ready for an assault from the authorities. He hadn't picked up anything on the drone to indicate that they were ready for trouble, but he liked to be prepared just in case. He figured that it had to do with him being a boy scout as a child and their motto was be prepared. So now, he was getting prepared.

Iron Phoenix was a problem, one that had origins going back to World War Two. They were a branch of former Nazis, now called Neo-Nazis by the current government. Ozzy had hated Nazis. His father had fought in World War Two against the Nazis and Hitler.

As he watched, Ozzy noticed that the compound was starting to come to life in a big way. Men with guns were moving to various posts around the interior of the compound and he spotted a flash of light from the roof. Shit. Snipers with nightscopes. Ozzy pulled out his cell phone and hit Riley's number on the speed dial!

~ ~ ~

Tel Aviv, Israel.

Nick Storm frowned as he watched the CCTV footage of the attack in the open-air market. Mac was sitting beside him and watching as well. Storm felt sick at his stomach as he watched the virus take hold of its victims and they began to convulse and die, gasping for breath as their lungs filled with blood. A few patients didn't die from it. It turned out that they were not Jewish.

"My God those people are monsters!" Mac gasped.

"Yes, they are," Storm agreed, his voice had gotten as cold and hard as a diamond.

"You two have approval to help me and my team go after Bern and his Iron Cross cronies," Ari informed them.

"I wouldn't miss it for the world," Storm hissed.

"Me either," Mac announced. Like Storm, she had also worked in the CIA's Special Activities Division before leaving the Agency and going freelance with her crew on *The Sea Chaser.*

~ ~ ~

Dieter Bern was making plans. He had three cannisters of the virus with him. His soldiers were preparing to take smaller delivery devices and spread out over Israel to infect the entire population. Bern was supervising the transfer of the weaponized virus from the cannisters into the smaller grenade like devices that would be used to spread the virus.

The leader of the Neo-Nazi group Iron Phoenix was proud of how well his plan had worked. Already terror was spreading across the capital city. Soon, a second attack would take place. If it proved as successful as the first attack, Tel Aviv would lock down under martial law. Already, police and military units were patrolling the city. That would already be making the general population somewhat nervous.

Terror was a specialty of Iron Phoenix. They had wreaked havoc across Europe and had enjoyed a few successes in the United States, however those had been quite costly for the organization. This time, Bern thought, this time Iron Phoenix would triumph!

Nick Storm had settled in the passenger seat as Ari had driven them out of the secret Mossad safehouse. Mac was in the backseat, wearing a vest and carrying an Uzi as well as her personal firearm. Nick had the same type of armament. They were ready for action.

Neither Nick nor Mac asked where they were headed. They figured that Ari knew where they were headed. Both were more concerned with stopping more terror attacks in Tel Aviv. That was why they were there. To stop Iron Phoenix once and for all!

~ ~ ~

Dieter Bern smiled as he watched his followers suit up in preparation for their strikes at the inferior creatures that enslaved the white man by controlling the banks around the world. The Jews were in every bank and board room, silently plotting to take over the world while they turned good men in pathetic sheep who would follow their orders blindly in an effort to feed their families.

He had been taught to hate Jews from birth. He was raised by parents who fired any Jew that managed to hire into any of their companies. According to his parents, the Jews were less than human, more like rabid beasts that needed to be put down. Not a single one of them should be allowed to live. Not man, woman, or child.

~ ~ ~

Washington, D.C.

Blake Dern was worried. D.C. was a town that ran on gossip and some was waiting on him when he returned home. Jack Riley was in town and he was supposed to be tracking down a link to Iron Phoenix and the Valhalla Virus. A little bird had let him know that his name had been mentioned to the President by Riley. Even though Riley's task force had been officially disbanded, Riley was still on the government payroll.

Senator Blake Dern needed to do something about that. Disgracing him wouldn't be enough. No, what he needed for Jack Riley was a far more permanent solution. Iron Phoenix had specialist that could be sent against Riley. Maybe it was time to call one of them in...

~ ~ ~

Jack Riley joined Ozzy outside the estate that Edgar Klausen had gone to. Riley wanted to eyeball the place before committing the FBI's Hostage Rescue Team and the D.C. SWAT team to a fire-fight. Because he was fairly certain that was what was going to happen. Riley knew better than to think about joining the operation himself. Those days were far behind him and he had learned that the hard way.

Running Caribe had made him soft. While he was working to get back into fighting shape, it was a long and tedious process. At least Jack Junior was a teenager now, though that brought on a whole new set of problems. He pushed that thought aside for another time. He couldn't afford to be distracted right now.

~ ~ ~

"I've got it," Tristan Sorenson said with a sigh.

"Got what?" Gina Torres asked.

"A vaccine that can defeat Valhalla," Sorenson said wearily.

"That's great. How soon can it be formulated?"

"About three hours. The CDC can transmit the formula to Israel and they can start inoculating their people as soon as possible.," Tristan told her. He tapped a key on the keyboard of the computer he was using. The formula was sent to the CDC.

"I wish that you hadn't done that," Gina sighed, her tone sad. Tristan turned to face her.

"What do you mean?" he asked.

"Because now I have to kill you," Gina replied driving an ink pen into his neck, poking a hole in his carotid artery. Tristan grabbed at his throat as Gina pulled the pen free. Blood fountained across the room. Gina gave him a sad smile. It was the last thing that Tristan Sorenson saw before he died.

Jack gave the signal and the assault teams moved in. He glanced at his watch. Time was running out. Iron Phoenix had to be stopped and it had to be done sooner than later!

Ozzy stayed with him, helping direct the assault team using a drone to seek out the defenders. Gunfire erupted in the darkness. The assault was on, but was it in time?

~ ~ ~

Atlanta, GA. CDC headquarters.

Gabriel Erskine opened the e-mail that had just popped up in his mailbox. It was from Tristan Sorenson. Erskine opened the e-mail and the attachment that had come with it. He started to read, then his eyes flew open wide. He snatched up his phone and dialed the White House.

Tel Aviv, Israel.

Ari's cell rang and he answered it at once. He listened for a few moments and then ordered the driver to head for a new destination. "What?" Nick asked, his gaze chilling.

"Just got word that Iron Phoenix is going for another soft target. If they manage, it could go down as the worst terrorist attack in Israeli history," Ari replied.

"We can't let that happen. What's the target?"

"Ofer Grand Mall Petach Tikva. Lots of people there this time of day, maybe a few thousand people there. We cannot let them spread this virus there," Ari told him.

"We have to get there first," Nick said.

"Agreed. We need a way to totally destroy the virus before it can be released or spread. Anybody got any ideas how to do that?" Ari asked.

Eighteen

Nick Storm frowned as he listened to Ari have all traffic routed towards the waterfront. Nick understood the why. The waterfront had fewer potential targets than the mall. Ari felt that if the terrorists couldn't reach the mall, they would have to head for the port. Because the seaport currently had three or four cruise ships that had just arrived and contained a wealth of potential targets for the genetically modified virus.

Nick had encountered Neo-Nazis on other missions, but he had never faced stakes like the ones he faced now. Sure, Operation Skyfire had been world-threatening but not on near the scale of the Valhalla virus. He wished that he could make the vehicle they were riding in go faster. Where were all the James Bond movie gadgets at when you really needed them?

~ ~ ~

Dieter Bern was angry. Their route to the original target had been cut off. Now they were headed for the alternate target where the cruise ships landed, with Mossad in close pursuit. This mission could not fail! Not if Iron Phoenix was to emerge as the savior of the world once Valhalla had been unleashed. No, the Valhalla Strike had to be successful! Bern refused to accept that there was any chance that it could fail.

The convoy in which he and his men were traveling could no longer reach the mall. All of the routes had been closed off by military forces. The seaport was the only other place where they could use Valhalla to claim the casualties that his father had asked for. Bern could not fail. To fail was to die!

~ ~ ~

Ari spotted the convoy first and stomped on the gas. A running fire-fight through the city streets wasn't an optimal plan, but it appeared that it was the best that they could hope for. They could not let Iron Phoenix release the virus. It was too deadly. "Get ready," Ari called as they sped closer to the Neo-Nazi convoy.

Nick leaned out of the passenger-side window, leveling his rifle at the convoy ahead of him. He aimed and fired, blowing the rear window out of the nearest SUV. The SUV fish-tailed briefly before multiple flashed of return fire blasted back at them. Nick fired again and one of the rear tires disintegrated in a flash of shredded rubber before the wheel it the street and started spraying sparks everywhere. Nick fired again, his bullets puncturing the gas tank. The sparks ignited the gas and fumes and detonated with a fiery boom that lifted the SUV into the air, engulfed in flames. Nick ducked back inside the vehicle as they blasted through the flames and wreckage.

"One down, four to go," Mac said as she leaned out her window and fired at the next vehicle.

"She makes it sound easy," Nick growled as he too slipped back into firing position.

"Of course, she does," Ari yelled, fighting to keep the remaining vehicles of the convoy in sight. The Israeli agent stepped on the gas, driving like a man possessed. Storm understood why. If those cannisters of the virus were released, the death toll would run into the millions. Extreme heat could destroy the virus. Because of that, Storm wasn't worried about the SUV that had blown up.

The ones they were pursuing were another matter. They could not let them release the virus. Bullets hammered at the bulletproof windshield of the Mossad vehicle. Storm leaned out and opened fire as Mac did the same from the other side. The gas tank exploded and sent the vehicle into the air. Ari raced past before it could crash down on them. Two down.

Suddenly, one of the SUV's split off and shot down a side street. Ari snarled a curse as he stayed on the trail of the two remaining vehicles. Mac got on the radio and sent out the name of the road that the vehicle had exited on. And gave the license plate so that others could intercept and stop the fleeing vehicle.

"We have got to get closer. We can let any of these guys get away with the virus," Storm growled.

"It's not like I am trying to let them get away," Ari snapped in response.

"Get me closer," Storm commanded as he scrambled out the window and onto the roof of the SUV.

"Nick, what the hell are you doing?" Mac screamed.

"Just get me closer!"

"I think I know what he's planning. This guy is fucking nuts!" Ari shouted as he stood on the gas pedal. They hit the bumper of the Iron Phoenix vehicle and Nick made his move. Storm launched himself onto the other vehicle's roof.

It hurt when he landed, but Nick had expected that. He grabbed ahold of one of the struts for the luggage rack and jammed the muzzle of his rifle down onto the roof, pulling the trigger and blasting a hole in the roof. The van swerved to the left towards a truck. Storm jumped an instant before it struck the other vehicle. He hit the pavement and rolled, slapping down with his arm as he rolled to help spread out the impact. A heartbeat later, both vehicles erupted in a gigantic fireball and windows up and down the street shattered.

Ari skidded to a halt beside him and Storm scrambled back into the van. Ari had it in motion before Storm shut the door. "Don't you ever do anything that stupid again, Nick!" Mac shouted from the seat behind him.

"I hope I don't have to," Storm told her, wincing as he moved bruised muscles.

"I have them in sight," Ari hissed from the driver's seat. Nick leaned out the window and aimed his rifle. Two shots snapped out and then the bolt locked over the empty chamber. Cursing he pulled the rifle in and slapped a fresh magazine place as Mac fired from the passenger side window. The Iron Phoenix vehicle fish-tailed as the bullets shredded the rear tires, sending the vehicle into a skid. The Iron

Phoenix soldiers exited the vehicle, spreading out like rats from a sinking ship.

Ari skidded to a stop and the three of them jumped out. Ari cut down two terrorists as Mac blaster two more. Nick cut down another. Dieter Bern ducked into a building. Nick chased him, skidding to a halt as the glass doors exploded outward, propelled by high velocity gunfire. Nick dropped and rolled, looking for a target. He got off a shot as Bern darted into an elevator and the doors slid closed. Nick pushed to his feet and ran inside. The elevator appeared to be headed towards the roof. He took a second elevator and pressed the button for the top floor.

It seemed to take forever for the elevator to rise. Nick prayed that it wouldn't stop before reaching the top floor. He glanced at his watch. This was taking too long! Finally, the elevator slowed and stopped on the top floor. Storm stabbed the open-door button and darted out into the hall as soon as the doors were open enough for him to get through them.

A bullet snapped past his head and he hit the floor and rolled. He triggered a burst towards the closing door that led to the stairs to the roof. Storm pushed to his feet and ran for the door. He threw it open, expecting gunfire but there was none. Storm raced up the stairs. Dammit! Bern had made it to the roof.

Storm threw the door open and dived onto the roof, rolling to try and take himself out of the line of fire. Nick rolled onto his knees, his rifle up in a firing position as he located Bern. The Neo-Nazi stood near the edge of the roof, one of the Valhalla cannisters in his hand. The other was on the lid, preparing twist it off. "You are too late, American. All the Jews are going to die!" Bern shouted.

"Not if I can help it," Storm whispered taking careful aim. He squeezed the trigger and Dieter Bern screamed as the hand holding the cannister exploded at the wrist, the cannister and hand falling to the ground. This time Bern's head exploded into a cloud of pink mist and his body tumbled over the edge of the building.

Slowly, Nick Storm pushed himself to his feet and walked over to the cannister. He removed the dead hand and headed back downstairs. Mac and Ari met him in the lobby. Nick handed the cannister to the Mossad agent. "I think this needs to be destroyed,"

Storm whispered. Then Mac was in his arms, hugging him as tight as she could.

~ ~ ~

It took a couple of days to get everything sorted out. Iron Phoenix was dead and gone for good. All of the members had been rounded up and were under arrest and sent to supermax prisons, thanks to Jack Riley and friends. The CDC had created the anti-virus and shipped it to Israel. Mac and Nick had spent a few days enjoying their stay in the country. They caught a ride back to the States on a military transport.

Mac would be returning to the *Sea Chaser*, and Nick was heading back to Key West. It appeared that Caribe had been given new life, though it would be a much more streamlined iteration. Jack would still be in charge, Dixon would handle the cyber end of things, and Nick would act as the lone agent looking into terrorist activities in the region.

Gina Torres had vanished without a trace. But Nick had a feeling that she would rear her head again. He planned to be there to put a bullet in her head when she did.

Thank you for reading.

Please review this book. Reviews
help others find Absolutely Amazing eBooks and
inspire us to keep providing these marvelous tales.
If you would like to be put on our email list
to receive updates on new releases,
contests, and promotions, please go to
AbsolutelyAmazingEbooks.com and sign up.

About the Author

Bill Craig is the best-selling author of more than 60 novels spread across the genres from mystery to pulp to science fiction to westerns. Bill is best known for his *Marlow Key West* mysteries and his *Mitch Cooper* mysteries. Bill often likes to say that it only took him 34 years to become an overnight success. And when introducing himself he adds that he kills people for a living, much like the fictional Rick Castle on television.

For sales, editorial information, subsidiary rights information
or a catalog, please write or phone or e-mail
AbsolutelyAmazingEbooks
Manhanset House
Shelter Island Hts., New York 11965-0342, US
Tel: 212-427-7139
www.AbsolutelyAmazingEbooks.com
bricktower@aol.com
www.IngramContent.com

For sales in the UK and Europe please contact our distributor,
Gazelle Book Services
White Cross Mills
Lancaster, LA1 4XS, UK
Tel: (01524) 68765 Fax: (01524) 63232
email: jacky@gazellebooks.co.uk